groucho Marx, King of the Jungle

Also by Ron Goulart

Groucho Marx, Secret Agent
Groucho Marx and the Broadway Murders
Elementary, My Dear Groucho
Groucho Marx, Private Eye
Groucho Marx, Master Detective

groucho Marx, King of the Jungle

Ron Goulart

Thomas Dunne Books
St. Martin's Minotaur 🐾 New York

THOMAS DUNNE BOOKS.
An imprint of St. Martin's Press.

GROUCHO MARX, KING OF THE JUNGLE. Copyright © 2005 by Groucho Marx
Productions Inc. and Ron Goulart. All rights reserved. Printed in the United
States of America. No part of this book may be used or reproduced in any
manner whatsoever without written permission except in the case of brief
quotations embodied in critical articles or reviews. For information,
address St. Martin's Press, 175 Fifth Avenue, New York, N.Y. 10010.

www.minotaurbooks.com

Library of Congress Cataloging-in-Publication Data

Goulart, Ron, 1933–
    Groucho Marx, king of the jungle : a mystery featuring Groucho Marx /
Ron Goulart.—1st ed.
        p. cm.
    ISBN 0-312-32216-X
    EAN 978-0-312-32216-8
    1. Marx, Groucho, 1891–1977—Fiction. 2. Hollywood (Los Angeles,
Calif.)—Fiction. 3. Motion picture industry—Fiction. 4. Screenwriters—
Fiction. 5. Jungle films—Fiction. 6. Comedians—Fiction. I. Title.

PS3557.O85G755 2005
813'.54—dc22

                                                    2004066412

First Edition: July 2005

10 9 8 7 6 5 4 3 2 1

To the Saturday lunch group. Or most of them anyway.

Thanks again to Robert Finkelstein
for his continued cooperation.

groucho Marx, King of the Jungle

One

I'd promised my wife that until our baby was born, I absolutely would not let Groucho Marx lure me into helping him out on any more murder cases. Not a single one.

But then, just three weeks before the estimated arrival date, she herself insisted that Groucho and I get to work on the jungle man mystery.

That was early in April of 1940. By that time, we'd earned a reputation as pretty successful amateur detectives. "By that time," according to Groucho, "our success had put not only the FBI to shame, but the local police, Scotland Yard, Gang Busters, and the Junior G-Men as well. In addition, when the Thin Man compared his moustache to mine, he sulked for well over a week and refused to eat a bite. That made him even thinner."

I'm Frank Denby, and before I changed into a scriptwriter, I was a crime reporter for the *Los Angeles Times.* I met Groucho back in 1937, while I was writing a radio show called *Groucho Marx, Master Detective* for him. Soon after that, we teamed up to prove that a young actress's "suicide" was actually a murder.

My wife is Jane Danner, the best-looking cartoonist in America. Her newspaper comic strip, *Hollywood Molly,* was continuing to pick up papers, and if I'd had an inclination to be a kept man, her income could've kept me very well.

Civilization in general wasn't in very good shape. World War II continued, and Hitler's armies had added Norway, Denmark, Belgium, and Holland to their list of conquered countries. The United States wasn't yet directly involved, but it looked like Congress would pass a Selective Service Act before 1940 was over. That would mean that a lot of guys would be drafted and that there'd be a greatly expanded Army when we finally did get into the war. Among the things that happened in Hollywood were Mickey Rooney once again getting voted the number-one box office attraction by the country's movie exhibitors, Lana Turner marrying Artie Shaw, and Bob Hope and Bing Crosby making their first *Road* picture.

Back in early February, I'd completed the second revision of my script for a jungle epic entitled *Ty-Gor and the Lost City.* They'd started shooting the picture out at Warlock Studios midway into March. Two weeks later yet another producer was brought in, and he decided, unlike his predecessor, that the movie needed more, not less, humor.

So he halted production for a few days, called me in, and had me add some new and funny scenes. In a rash moment I suggested that he might invite Groucho to do a walk-on. The producer loved the notion, so I came up with two short scenes for an African explorer named J. Darwin Underbrush.

That's why Groucho and I were walking along a wide, sunlit street on the Warlock grounds on the morning that the corpse was discovered on Soundstage 3.

A warm breeze was rattling the fronds of the rows of tall palm trees that lined the studio street. The side door of Soundstage 2 slid open, and about a dozen pretty platinum blondes in considerably condensed sailor suits started trooping out.

As they came straggling toward us, one of them, on spotting Groucho, did a take and then left the group to come hurrying up to us. "Would you be Groucho Marx?" she asked him, somewhat breathlessly.

Groucho considered the question, thoughtfully stroking his chin. "Actually I'd rather be somebody else," he told the blonde. "Give me some other suggestions."

Taking off her sailor hat, she held it, timidly, out toward him. "Will you, please, sign this, Mr. Marx?"

He accepted the proffered hat. "I usually have my attorneys peruse anything I'm asked to sign," he said, taking a blue fountain pen from the breast pocket of his multicolored sports coat. "But I can tell that you're an honest and upright young lady. Which, alas, rules you out for my purposes." He inscribed his name on the edge of the white hat.

"We're all in the chorus of a new musical," the girl explained. "It's called *Hot Tamales Join the Navy.*"

"Indeed?" He returned her hat. "I'd assumed that Balanchine was here filming a new version of *Swan Lake.*"

She smiled. "That's what I like about you, Mr. Marx."

"Which?"

"Your ready wit."

"Actually, my wit won't be ready until late next week," he informed her. "In the meantime, you'll have to put up with a few feeble jests I've pilfered from Joe Penner."

By this time, most of the other ladies of the chorus had realized who Groucho was, and he devoted the next ten minutes or so to autographing hats and, in one case, a dancer's brassiere.

"Being beloved," remarked Groucho as we continued on our way, "can be a great burden, Rollo."

3

"I've noticed."

"Now then, clarify this situation once again," he requested, putting his fountain pen away and producing a fresh cigar. "I am not wanted as the star of this jungle epic?"

"If you were the star, you'd be playing Ty-Gor and not Professor J. Darwin Underbrush."

"Then basically your producer chum is intending to talk to me about undertaking a *bit* part?" He unwrapped the cigar.

"Basically."

"Although MGM has seen fit to delete the fact from my official studio bio, I was asked to try out for the role of that other jungle lord, Tarzan."

"With what result?"

"When I first appeared in my leopard-skin costume, there was considerable swooning," he replied. "Even some of the female observers fainted away. I might still have snagged the role if those darned elephants hadn't stampeded after getting a look at me."

I nodded. "Well, as I already explained, this is a walk-on. Thing is," I reminded him, "they're offering you a handsome fee."

Lighting his cigar, he said, "Splendid, Rollo, since I'm so dreadfully tired of the ugly fees I've been handed of late."

"So this morning all we have to do is talk to Joel Farber."

"And he's the producer of this epic?"

"At the moment, yeah. And . . . Huh, that's odd."

"Are you alluding to that curly-haired young chap who's running heck-for-leather toward yon soundstage?"

"Yeah, that's Joel Farber himself."

"My, what a delightful coincidence."

* * *

4

Just inside the metal soundstage door, a uniformed studio guard stepped out of the shadows and into our path, swinging up his left hand in a stop-right-there gesture. His right hand was hovering over his holstered .38 revolver. "Sorry, fellas, no one is allowed in here just . . . Oh, hi, Frank."

"Howdy, Hal. What's going on?"

About two hundred yards away, near the indoor jungle set, several more guards and a few executives were huddled. The overhead lights in that area were on, and Joel Farber was heading in that direction.

"Bad accident," answered Hal.

"What happened?"

The guard shook his head. "Nobody's filled me in yet," he replied. "But it looks like Randy Spellman's been injured."

"Jesus," I observed. Spellman was the star of the damned movie.

"Since you're working on this Ty-Gor flicker, Frank, I guess you can go in. But about your pal here, I'm dubious."

"If I were either Smith or Dale," said Groucho, "I'd now say, 'Pleased to meet you, Mr. Dubious.' Since I'm not, I won't."

The lean guard chuckled. "Oh, you're Groucho Marx. I didn't recognize you without your moustache."

Slapping his palm against his upper lip, Groucho said, "I declare, that's the third time this week it's wandered off. And last year it flew south for the winter without so much as a—"

"Let us go chat with Joel and find out what's up." Taking hold of Groucho by the sleeve of his polychromous sports coat, I led him off to the brightly illuminated jungle.

Parked near the stretch of imitation and transplanted jungle foliage was a large mobile dressing room. As we drew closer, we saw that the aluminum door hung wide open and that light was spilling out from inside.

At the bottom of the short portable stairway, a body was sprawled, that of a big man wearing a leopard-skin loincloth and an open pale yellow robe. There were two blood-rimmed bullet holes in his broad, shaved chest.

"We seem, Franklin," said Groucho as we halted a few feet from the scatter of observers, "to have once again walked in on the ground floor of a murder."

"Yeah, and that's definitely Randy Spellman, the guy who's playing Ty-Gor."

"I deduced as much from the chap's fur-lined skivvies," he said. "Keep in mind, my boy, that we've both promised the fair Jane that there'll be absolutely no more amateur sleuthing for the nonce. Or for the nuns either."

"I know," I said, still frowning at Spellman's body. "We'll just wait until we can talk to Joel, then take our leave."

Groucho glanced toward the mobile dressing room. "Apparently somebody shot our jungle man while he was standing in the doorway, facing inward," he observed. "He then toppled down the steps to land flat on his tuchus, where he now lies."

"No amateur sleuthing," I reminded.

"Forgive me, Rollo. But I seem to have detecting in my blood," said Groucho. "Which may explain why I turn that unsightly shade of lavender when exposed to too much sun."

"All we'll do is wait for a chance to let Joel know we're here. Our meeting will have to be postponed."

"I'll struggle manfully to curb my private-eye impulses," he promised. "I'll also try to curb my St. Bernard. I have to admit, however, that I haven't been too successful at the latter chore and that the Beverly Hills city fathers, so I'm told, have sent away for a rail to ride me out of town on. On top of that, a preacher from the Church of the Latter Day Chores has been—"

"Frank." Joel Farber had noticed me and was heading over. "Hey, and you brought Groucho along." The producer shook Groucho's hand enthusiastically. "You're looking terrific, Groucho."

"Yes, I've been looking that way ever since I started soaking myself in Lux Flakes."

Chortling, Joel led us over to the side of the trailer. Lined up beside it were two rows of ten large wooden tubs each in which rested small palm trees planted in dirt and pine shavings. "Talk to my secretary about rescheduling our meeting," he said. "Obviously our movie's going to be delayed."

"I figured as much. What happened to Randy?"

Joel gave a moderate shrug. "A guard spotted the poor bastard flat on his ass over there about an hour ago."

"Nobody heard anything?" asked Groucho. "Gunshots? A quarrel?"

The curly-haired producer shook his head. "If anybody did, Groucho, I haven't heard about it yet."

I asked, "Have you notified the police?"

"Not yet, but we'll be calling the Studio City cops."

"Any idea," inquired Groucho, "why somebody would want to knock Spellman off? Other than anyone who's seen him act."

Joel said, "Could be somebody wanted to sabotage our movie."

"If they wanted to do that, they'd have left Spellman alive."

"Randy was a *putz*," admitted Joel. "Quite a few people, especially husbands of the dames he's fooled around with, hated the guy." He shrugged again, then looked thoughtfully from me to Groucho. "Say, wait a minute. You two guys have a pretty

7

good reputation as amateur detectives. Suppose we hire you to look into this business?"

"We're temporarily retired from the gumshoe business," I told my producer.

Groucho added, "We've taken a vow not to return to ratiocination for a spell. I've also taken a vow of celibacy, and that one I'm willing to break. But I don't see how that applies to this situation."

Taking hold of my arm, Joel invited, "Well, at least come back over and take a gander at the body."

I turned toward Groucho.

He said, "We can at least do that."

So we went and gazed down at the corpse.

There weren't any powder burns on Spellman's chest, meaning that whoever shot him hadn't been standing very close to him. Making a rough guess, judging from the condition of the body, I figured he'd been killed sometime last night.

I was mentioning that to Groucho, in a near whisper, when a pudgy, sunburned guy in his late twenties made his way, avoiding assorted cables and wires on the soundstage floor, over to join the group circling the dead man.

"Damn it, this means another delay," he said to nobody in particular. "My dad, you know, hasn't been any too happy with the way this film is dragging—"

"Take it easy, Jack," advised Joel, moving over to the young man and putting a hand on the shoulder of his checked sports coat. "Randy's been killed, and I'm sure your father can't blame us for that."

"Spellman shouldn't have been in this new Ty-Gor at all. He's . . . he was too old and too flabby for the part. Besides, the guy was, in my dad's opinion, a second-rate . . . make that a third-rate actor."

Groucho leaned nearer to me. "This sun-dried lad is the off-spring of whom exactly?" he inquired quietly.

"That's Jack Benson," I explained. "He's the son of Arthur Wright Benson, the creator of Ty-Gor and author of all the many beloved novels about the king of the jungle."

"How come they allow the little tyke on the set? You wrote the script and—"

"It's in his dad's contract with Warlock that a representative of Arthur Wright Benson, Inc., shall be allowed to observe all aspects of the production of any Ty-Gor motion picture. Jack's basically a nitwit, but relatively harmless. And he seems to like my script."

"I knew he must have one redeeming feature."

". . . On the previous Ty-Gor film," Jack Benson was telling our producer, "the then producer had the good sense to do most of the jungle shooting on my dad's private jungle out at Rancho Tygoro in the Valley."

"We're on a tighter budget on this one, Jack."

"Well, *Ty-Gor's Jungle Mystery* did terrifically at the box office," young Benson continued. "That was in spite of the mediocre performance—make that a lousy performance by Spellman." He pointed down at the deceased actor with a thumb.

"Whatever happened to the quaint old custom of speaking well of the dead?" inquired Groucho.

Squinting at him, Jack asked, "Who are you?"

"Merely an unemployed muscle man who dropped by to audition for the position of Spellman's stand-in," Groucho told Arthur Wright Benson's only son. "And I really think I can handle

9

it, since it seems to require nothing more than lying on my back and looking vacant. I've been doing that for years without realizing a chap could earn—"

"Oh, you're one of those Marx Brothers."

"Two of those Marx Brothers actually. Plus one of the Brontë Sisters."

Making an annoyed sound, Jack turned again to Joel Farber. "Who killed Spellman?"

"That we don't know. We only discovered the poor guy's body about—"

"Instead of everyone's standing around shedding crocodile tears," Jack said, "let's look around and find out what really happened here." He started toward the dead man's trailer. "We'll probably find something in his dressing room to tell us—"

"Whoa," I suggested. "Not a good idea, Jack."

He frowned at me. "You're the scriptwriter, Denby," he said, "not the head of Warlock studios. So it's not your—"

"Frank's right." Joel caught up with him, took hold of his arm, and slowed him down. "The police won't want anybody nosing around in Randy's dressing room until they've gone over it."

Sighing, miming exasperation, the sunburned Jack said, "Okay, all right. I can tell you right now that my father's not going to be pleased by any of this."

"We're not all that pleased ourselves," Joel assured him.

Two

Groucho and I were about a half a block from Moonbaum's Delicatessen on Sunset, when a plump middle-aged woman in a flowered print dress stepped into our path.

She gave Groucho a flustered smile, held out a green-covered autograph album toward him. "I just love the Marx Brothers," she informed him.

"That's more than the Marx Brothers do." He took the book, reached inside my jacket with his free hand to borrow my fountain pen.

The woman watched him intently as he signed his name on a blank page. "You look," she said, "older in real life."

"*This* is real life?" His eyebrows climbed. "Thanks for the warning." He returned her album, put my pen in his coat pocket, and we continued on our way.

"Three," I remarked.

"I'd be inclined to agree with you, my lad, if I knew what in the dickens you were nattering about."

"That's three of my pens you've appropriated so far this month."

"Let me know when it reaches five."

In front of Moonbaum's the aging newsboy was holding up an Extra edition of the *LA Times.* "Brutal Hollywood slaying!" he was hollering. "Ty-Gor murdered in movie jungle!"

Groucho said, "We'll ignore this."

I said, "We won't even buy a paper."

"Ty-Gor slaughtered on movie set!" added the newsboy. "Blonde girlfriend sought by police!"

We both halted.

"Loan me the price of a paper," Groucho requested.

"My treat." I bought a copy of the newspaper.

Nodding at Groucho, the paper vendor said, "In my humble opinion, Groucho, the last Marx Brothers movie wasn't very funny."

Groucho narrowed one eye. "My dear chap. *At the Circus* wasn't intended to be funny at all," he explained. "After Zeppo deserted us, Chico, Harpo, and I decided that we're really trage-dians and not silly buffoons. You shouldn't have laughed at all."

"I didn't laugh much."

"I accept your apology." Groucho made his way into the restaurant, moving toward his regular booth at the rear.

I followed, trying to read the front-page story about Spell-man's murder while walking.

When I slid in across the green booth from Groucho, he asked, "And who is the golden-haired lass the law is seeking?"

Spreading the folded paper out on the green-topped table in front of me, I said, "Before we go into that, Groucho, allow me to point out that the *Times* quotes the noted movie mogul Joel Farber as saying that while he has full confidence in the Studio City police, Warlock has also retained the services of the distin-guished investigative team of Groucho Marx and Frank Denby."

"Distinguished, am I? By golly, nobody's called me that since . . . well, actually nobody's ever called me that," he admitted. "Must be my hanging around with the likes of you, Franklin, that's improved my reputation. Now if I can just find something to improve my complexion and give it that school-girl—"

"Be that as it may, I just hope Jane doesn't see this before I can talk to her," I cut in. "After I promised her I wouldn't—"

"My boy, she happens to be married to an erstwhile *Los Angeles Times* reporter and is therefore well aware that they are all a passel of lying louts." Groucho made a dismissive gesture. "Now tell me about the platinum-tressed tootsie in the case."

"So you fellows are playing detective again, huh?" Millman the waiter placed two glasses of water down on our table.

"We are not," countered Groucho. "What we've been playing is Puss in the Corner."

"Ask me, the dame did it," observed the gaunt waiter. "This is a crime of passion if there ever was one."

"Can you take your mind off this sordid matter long enough to take my order for a pastrami sandwich, my good man?"

"I already put in your order, Groucho, minute I saw you come sauntering in," answered Millman. "And blueberry blintzes for your Watson here."

"Very well, you have my permission to begone."

"Who do you think bumped the poor galoot off?"

"My esteemed partner here—not to mention the esteemed clams in your kitchen—my esteemed partner and I no longer handle murder cases. We limit our practice to finding stray dogs. And small, docile dogs at that."

Millman sighed. "I was hoping it wasn't true."

"What, that we've given up—"

13

"No, that you'd lost your sense of humor entirely. But it's obvious that—"

"Absent yourself."

Our waiter went shuffling away.

Groucho rested his elbows on the table. "So who was that lady?"

"This doesn't make any sense, Groucho." I frowned, shaking my head. "The police want to talk to Dorothy Woodrow."

"She's a stuntwoman, is she not?"

"Yeah, she worked on the last Ty-Gor movie and was stunting on this one, too," I answered. "Nice girl, in her late twenties, pretty."

"I believe I've encountered Miss Woodrow in the past, but I strive not to become too interested in women who're stronger than I am." He was leaning forward, reading the paper upside down. "Says here she was having a steamy love affair with the late Randy Spellman."

"Naw, that was over months ago."

Reaching across the tabletop, Groucho picked up the *Times.* "Seems she signed in at the studio gate yesterday morning, but never signed out," he said. "Nary a soul has seen her since, and she's not at her place of residence in Manhattan Beach."

I shook my head again. "Dorothy's too smart to do anything like murdering Spellman."

"If she's really smart, why'd she ever tie up with a lunkhead like Spellman?"

"Love is strange."

"Come to think of it, Evangeline, I've noticed that myself."

Millman arrived with our orders, delivering them silently and departing.

I took the *Times* back, turning to the continuation of the murder story on page 3. "This makes even less sense," I said after scanning the column. "The police say they found a note from Dorothy in Spellman's dressing room trailer."

"Saying what?"

"Saying, and I quote, 'Randy—I warned you that you can't get away with this! You'd better meet me tonight in your trailer at 7:30—or you'll be very sorry! (Signed) Dot.'"

"Very forceful prose style," observed Groucho. "Was this typed, handwritten, or illuminated?"

Folding up the newspaper, I deposited it beside me on the bench. "The police didn't say."

"We'll have to find out then and . . . oops, forgive me, Rollo. For a moment I thought we were back in the gumshoe trade."

"But since we're not, we don't have to worry about the note," I said as I picked up my fork. "And you won't have to cudgel your brain about clues."

"Pity in a way, since I just purchased a set of matched cudgels." His face, briefly, assumed a forlorn expression.

"But it is too bad the cops think that Dorothy is a woman scorned. That she shot the guy and slipped off the lot somehow."

"In spite of her love note, I don't doubt that there are many other women, as well as men, children, and a few selected chimpanzees, who had good reasons for wanting to send Spellman off to glory," said Groucho. "However, young sir, since I am dedicated, as I fortunately just recalled in the nick of time, to keeping you crime-free for the next few weeks, I must now call this gruesome discussion to a close." He picked up his kosher dill, took a bite. "I am officially changing the subject. Now then, are you and the missus still stubbornly refusing to name your forthcoming son Groucho in my honor?"

"Jane's absolutely certain the baby is going to be a girl."

"Then how about Grouchoella?"

"Nope."

"Grouchorita? Little Bo Groucho?"

"Not likely."

Undaunted, he went on to contribute several more suggestions.

Three

When I crossed the threshold of our beach house in Bayside, a growling commenced in Jane's studio.

"Shut up, dopey," she said.

"I haven't said a word," I called out.

"That remark was addressed to Dorgan," said my wife. "It's the master of the ménage, Dorgan, so you don't have to defend me."

I, somewhat gingerly, crossed the living room. Our retired bloodhound peered out of the studio at me. Apparently I passed inspection, and Dorgan started wagging his tail.

"He's gotten increasingly protective." I halted in the doorway. "And, hey, aren't you supposed to rest about this time?"

Jane was seated at her drawing board, a number-one brush in her hand. "Speaking of being overly protective," she said, smiling.

"And where's your assistant?"

"She had a dentist appointment," Jane answered. "I'm only inking in the main characters on a *Hollywood Molly* Sunday page. Nothing strenuous, Frank."

Dorgan flopped down in front of me, rolled over on his back.

Crouching, I rubbed his stomach. "You can work later, Jane. I really think you ought to rest, take a nap."

"Can't nap," she said. "We're expecting company shortly."

"Who?"

"Enery."

I straightened up. "I'll have to tell him the Ty-Gor movie's going to be delayed," I said, frowning. "See, Spellman was murdered this morning, but don't worry, because even though Groucho and I walked in on the—"

"I know about Spellman's death. Enery told me over the phone."

"That why he's coming over?"

Jane held out her hand to me, and I helped her dismount from her chair. As I kissed her on the cheek, she said, "He's got a problem he wants to talk over."

"Enery mention what sort of problem?"

"Well," said Jane, smoothing out her polka-dot maternity smock, "it's going to involve your breaking a promise to me."

"Hum?"

Walking around the sprawled Dorgan, she said, "The one about you and Groucho not being detectives for a while."

"C'mon, Jane, you're less than three weeks from having our baby."

She settled herself on our living room sofa. "Even so, I think it'd be a swell idea if you fellows took an interest in this Randolph Spellman murder case."

"Nope, no. Whenever I've been involved with a murder case over the past few years, you've worried," I pointed out. "So at a time like this I sure as hell don't intend to get into any dangerous situation that can—"

"You and Groucho can more than likely solve the whole

mess in a week or less," she said confidently, taking hold of my hand and pulling me down to sit beside her. "That'll leave you with plenty of time to fret, pace the floor, and do all the other things expectant fathers are required to do. Really, Frank, you don't have to worry about me."

I attempted a scowl. "Why exactly are you so eager to have us take up this particular case, Jane?"

"I told you. Because of Enery McBride."

I gave up on the scowl. "How does he tie in, outside of playing the cannibal chief in the damn movie?"

"Well, it has to do with the stuntwoman."

"With Dorothy Woodrow?"

Jane nodded. "Yes."

"You know the cops are looking for Dorothy? She used to be Spellman's girlfriend, and she seems to have written him a threatening note. They suspect she shot the guy."

"Enery is certain she didn't shoot Spellman."

"How come?"

"Because for the past three months or so she's been *his* girlfriend," Jane replied.

After glancing again at his wristwatch, Enery McBride asked, "You sure you want to get involved in this, Frank?"

Before I could answer, Jane said, "We're both sure, Enery."

He nodded in my direction. "Frank?"

"Tell us about Dorothy," I suggested.

Our actor friend was sitting on the edge of an armchair, facing us, hunched slightly forward. "What worries me most," he admitted, "is that I haven't heard from Dorothy. According to the newspapers, the police seem to believe she's hiding out someplace." He shook his head. "But I'm not sure about that."

"Why not?"

"She'd have telephoned," he answered, "or gotten in touch with me some way. I'm afraid that whoever killed that bastard Spellman may've hurt Dorothy, too."

I told him, "If she was shot when Randy was, they'd have left her there."

"Maybe she was taken along as a hostage or—"

"You wouldn't need a hostage to sneak out of the Warlock studios in the middle of the night."

"Whatever happened, Frank, she's disappeared." He made a forlorn sound. "When I talked to Jane, she said you and Groucho might be able to help find her. Trouble is, there's not much more I can do openly."

"What about talking to the police?" I asked him.

He smiled ruefully. "We've all been avoiding something," Enery said. "If I walk into the Studio City police station to ask about Dorothy—all they're going to say is, 'How come this colored boy is interested in a white girl?' "

"You're right, yeah," I admitted. "What about her friends—have you talked to them?"

Getting up, slowly, he walked over to a window to look out toward the ocean downhill. "I suppose I should've told you about Dorothy and me earlier," he said. "But we—well, Dorothy especially—decided to keep our relationship quiet. Sometimes the studios can be . . ." He shrugged, still staring out at the late-afternoon Pacific. "Especially in her case. I got to know her when we were both working on the last Ty-Gor movie, while it was shooting out at the private jungle that the writer has in the Valley."

"Rancho Tygoro," said Jane. "Arthur Wright Benson, who writes the Ty-Gor books, has a ten-acre jungle on his estate. The guy collects tropical plants and foliage."

"And obviously he makes more money off jungle men than I do," I said. "About Dorothy's friends, Enery?"

"The point is—well, we liked each other," he said. "We started, you know, seeing each other. But mostly at her place in Manhattan Beach and my cottage in San Amaro. Nobody was going to spot us at the Coconut Grove." He turned his back to the window. "Anyway, only a couple of Dorothy's friends even know about us. I've only been able to get in touch with one of them so far, and she doesn't know any more than I do." He returned to the armchair, checking his watch again. "Jesus, Dorothy's been missing since last night."

"We'll find her," I assured him, hoping I sounded confident.

Jane asked, "Why'd you refer to Spellman as a bastard?"

"I could just as easily have said son of a bitch." Enery sat down again. "Dorothy was involved with him for a couple of months last year. It took her that long to find out what sort of louse he was. Then she quit seeing him."

"The police have the notion she was still in love with the guy," I reminded. "That note Dorothy allegedly wrote him establishes that point—far as the cops are concerned."

"Bullshit," Enery said. "She never wrote the letter. Dorothy hadn't communicated with Spellman in any way for months. And she never called herself Dot."

My wife asked, "Did any of the papers print a photo of the actual letter?"

"No, only quoted from it," I answered. "And nobody's said anything about comparing the handwriting—if the thing is handwritten—to a sample of her writing."

"Can we get a look at it?"

"Probably," I replied. "I know a couple of guys on the Studio City force who can maybe get me a copy."

Enery was looking yet again at his watch. Rubbing his fingertips across the crystal, he said, "There's another reason the police have linked her with Spellman. The guy hated to admit any girl had walked out on him. I know for a fact that he's been telling people Dorothy was still carrying the torch."

"Do you know," asked Jane, "if she was anywhere near him last night?"

"Not sure, damn it," he replied.

"Wouldn't she have told you?"

"I only talked to her for a few minutes yesterday, while she was getting ready to double for Marlene Tubridy," Enery said. "Dorothy was supposed to drop over to my place last night, but she said something had come up. Something important."

"You don't know what it was?" I asked.

"Nope. She seemed—upset, uneasy. She only told me it was nothing for me to worry about," Enery explained. "We never have long conversations on the set, so I didn't have time to find out any more."

"It could've had something to do with Spellman," I said.

"I just really don't know, Frank."

Jane remembered her coffee cup, picked it up, took a very brief sip. "Did Spellman know about you and Dorothy?"

"He might have."

"And he might have been riding her."

"If Spellman knew, he'd have been nasty, sure."

"Which could be why she went to see him."

"Yeah, but that's not a good-enough reason for Dorothy to kill the guy."

I asked, "Who are her two friends that you can trust?"

"One's a bit player who lives in Hollywood, name's Margery Corke." Enery gave me her address and phone number. "She's out near Palm Springs on location for a few days. But I was able to get hold of her on the telephone. Margery claims she doesn't know a darn thing. Other's guy, stuntman named Randy Cox. Does a lot of B Westerns and is a very enthusiastic Communist. Dorothy and I have been to a few parties of his down in Venice. Randy I haven't been able to get in touch with yet. I'm planning to check some of the bars he hangs out at."

"How about any of Dorothy's friends who don't know about you, Enery?" asked Jane. "We can try them, explaining that Frank's working for the Warlock studios. Possibly one of them knows something about where she is."

"Not a bad idea." Enery took the notepad Jane handed him, thought for a moment, and then started writing. "I know of three others."

"So what we have to do is find Dorothy," I said, "and figure out who really killed Spellman." I tried to imply that this would be a snap to bring off, but I didn't quite succeed.

"Judging by your track record," said Enery, "I think you can do it." He handed Jane the notebook.

I got to my feet. "And you don't mind if Groucho helps out, too?"

Enery grinned faintly. "You're a team, aren't you? Sure, I want the whole set of detectives." He left the chair, moving toward the door. "I'm going to try to track down Randy Cox, see if he's got any idea where Dorothy is."

I went along with him, opened the door. A thin mist had been drifting in from the late-afternoon Pacific.

Enery held out his hand, and we shook. "You can leave a message with my answering service, soon as you find out anything." He turned and went hurrying away into the blurred afternoon.

Four

I can carry coffee cups into the kitchen," Jane assured me.

"No, you rest, and I'll do it," I said, getting up. "As I recall, that was part of the marriage vows. Love, honor, and carry coffee cups."

"Hooey," observed my wife, but remained on the sofa.

I took two cups and saucers out to the kitchen, came back for the third. "Enery didn't drink much of his coffee. Too upset, I guess."

"Either that, or he happened to taste the coffee."

Cup in hand, I inquired, "Are you implying that the coffee I brewed wasn't up to snuff?"

"As snuff it was fine, but as coffee . . ."

"You're showing symptoms of Grouchoitis," I pointed out.

"There's no reason," she said, "why I can't, even in my delicate condition, make a darn pot of coffee."

When I returned from the kitchen, I settled into the chair Enery'd occupied. "I don't mean, Jane, to treat you like an invalid," I told her. "Maybe I'm being overly cautious, but that's because—"

"I know, Frank. It's okay," she said. "Let's talk about Enery."

"I'll call Groucho. Pretty sure he wants to work on this case."

"You've got two basic problems. Or three, if you count Groucho."

I nodded. "As I said to Enery—we have to find out what's become of Dorothy Woodrow, and we've got to track down the real murderer."

Jane asked, "You don't think Dorothy might actually have killed Spellman?"

"Doubt it, although that might turn out to be the situation," I answered. "I don't know her anywhere near as well as Enery does, but I don't think she's capable of killing anybody."

"Neither do I. Even so, you'd best keep an open mind."

"Actually, my mind's already closed for the season, but I'll do the best I can." I moved to the telephone on the end table.

"After you talk to him," said Jane, "we try those other friends of Dorothy's and see if they know anything."

"Or if they'll tell us."

Jane's slim shoulders rose and fell, and she sighed. "It's really damned stupid."

"Which?"

"That Enery and Dorothy can't even openly get together. That she's afraid to let all her friends know she's in love with him."

"Apparently you haven't noticed," I said as I picked up the receiver, "—in many ways it's a stupid world."

"I had noticed that, yes," she said. "So call Groucho."

Groucho himself answered the phone at his Beverly Hills home. "Shadrach's Kosher Pet Shop, offering the only Yiddish-speaking parrots in all of Greater Los Angeles. Mr. Shadrach is attending to the furnace, but I'll be absolutely delighted to serve you."

"Groucho, how'd you like to investigate the Spellman killing?"

"That would both thrill and delight me, but, alas, I fear the wrath of your dear wife," he replied. "I'm also a little wary of the Grapes of Wrath, although I find the Bananas of Wrath quite tasty."

"Jane is the one who first suggested we take up the case."

"Well then, Rollo, I'm glad you called," said Groucho. "Because I've been champing at the bit ever since we encountered that defunct jungle lord this morning. I don't know if you've ever champed at a bit, but they have a decidedly metallic taste and are nowhere near as flavorful as, say, pastrami or lox. Unfortunately, one can't go around saying, 'I'm champing at the lox,' unless one is perhaps understudying Georgie Jessel in a revival of *The Jazz Singer.* What caused Jane to change her mind?"

"Our friend Enery McBride." I gave Groucho the details of Enery's recent visit.

When I'd finished, Groucho suggested, "We'd best get together at my office on Sunset tomorrow to work out our plan of action. Meantime I'll do some cogitating. I may even have time for a little thinking."

"What time tomorrow?"

"Be there at the crack of dawn," he instructed. "And keep in mind, Watso, that dawn doesn't crack in that part of Hollywood until about 11 A.M."

27

Five

When Groucho emerged from Moonbaum's the next morning, he later told me, the middle-aged newsboy was shouting a new headline, " 'Police Still Hunting for Scorned Woman in Jungle King Murder!' "

Groucho took a copy of the newspaper. "Do you have change for a dime, my good man?"

"You trying to steal that cheapskate routine from Jack Benny?"

"No, I really am a cheapskate." He handed him a dime. "But if you don't spread it around, you can keep the whole ten cents."

Tucking the paper under his arm, Groucho braved the traffic on Sunset. He was aimed at the building, which resembled something left over from *Gone with the Wind,* that housed his office.

Just before he reached the entryway, a plump woman in a flower-print dress hailed him. "Mr. Marx, will you sign my book?"

"It all depends on the book," he replied. "I won't sign *Mein Kampf* or *The Trail of the Lonesome Pine,* but I'm sort of partial to *Nancy Drew and the Haunted Delicatessen* and *The Many Loves of—*"

"No, I mean my autograph book." She, a bit timidly, held out a green-covered signature album toward him.

"Why didn't you say so in the first place?" He whipped out the fountain pen he'd swiped from me and scrawled his name across a blank page. "And, dear lady, to quash for good and all the rumors that I'm a tightwad, you may keep this fountain pen. It's sure to become a souvenir that you'll cherish for all your born days. Or even longer if you so desire."

A bit perplexed, the woman took the album and my pen. "Why thank you, Mr. Marx."

"The next time somebody tells you that Groucho Marx is a cheapskate, you can tell them where to get off," he advised. "Myself, I always like to tell them to get off at the corner of Hollywood and Vine, but you may have another intersection you're fonder of." Bowing, he went bounding gracefully up the stairway to the second floor.

His secretary was seated at the reception desk, reading a newspaper.

"Had I but known," said Groucho, "I could have saved a dime."

Nan Somerville was a muscular woman in her late thirties. The fact that she'd been a circus acrobat and a stuntwoman at MGM had convinced Groucho she was ideally suited to be his secretary. Fortunately, she was also a crackerjack typist.

"Good morning, Groucho. I don't believe any of this malarkey about Dorothy Woodrow."

"And well you shouldn't. Do you know the lass?"

"Sure, she did some stunt work over at MGM while I was still there; nice kid. Are you and Frank really working on this Spellman case?"

Perching on the edge of the desk, he answered, "Yes,

Nanette, once again the greatest detective team since Gallagher and Sheen is back in business."

"Gallagher and Sheen weren't detectives."

"Even so."

Nan said, "I thought you and Frank were laying off this sort of thing until after the baby arrives."

"Jane has given us her permission to take up the investigation," Groucho informed his secretary. "And while we're at it, we're going to take up the hall carpet as well."

Resting both palms on the newspaper spread out on her desk, Nan asked, "Do you have any idea as to where Dorothy might be?"

"Nary a one." He took a fresh cigar from the pocket of his strawberry-colored sports coat. "Although Frank may have some fresh information when he arrives—he's due any moment now. We've committed ourselves to finding the lady, as well as the solution to the murder case."

"I haven't run into Dorothy for a couple of years or more," said Nan. "Suppose the police find her before you guys do?"

"Then I'd feel most chagrined." He lit his stogie. "Of course, I'd first look up *chagrined* in the dictionary to find out what it actually means. For all I know, I'm already feeling chagrined and have for years. Know anything about the late jungle man?"

Nan said, "I'd bet that one of his hobbies killed him."

Groucho's eyebrows rose. "Such hobbies as?"

"He was a womanizer and—"

"I used to be a harmonizer, though I don't suppose that's the same thing. And once I had myself simonized, but—"

". . . and an adulterer," his secretary continued. "Oh, and he was also an amateur photographer."

Exhaling smoke, Groucho inquired, "Specializing in the sort

of snapshots that people weren't anxious to share with their friends and neighbors?"

"That sort of stuff, yeah."

"My, you'd think a fellow with all those admirable traits would have been ideally suited for life in Hollywood and environs."

"He was, until yesterday," said Nan. "Friend of mine, Jason Brinker, who used to double for Spellman, told me the guy even got in some kind of squabble with Alicia Benson while they were shooting out at Rancho Tygoro on the last Ty-Gor flicker. She's Benson's only daughter."

"A romantic squabble?"

"More a quarrel of some kind. Jason never found out what exactly it was all about."

"Delving into Spellman's past," observed Groucho, "sounds like it's going to be jolly fun for one and all." He glanced toward the doorway, cupping a hand to his ear. "But hark, I believe I hear the approach of Franklin on little cat feet."

A moment later I entered the office.

Seated behind his desk in his private office, Groucho said, "According to the morning papers, Dorothy Woodrow is still at large."

"We can't even be certain she's still alive," I said.

"Come, come, Pollyanna, let's look on the bright side."

"Which is?"

After considering the buff-colored ceiling for a few seconds, Groucho replied, "Come to think of it, there isn't a bright side. If the young lady isn't on the wrong side of the Pearly Gates, then she's a fugitive from justice. Which is better than being a fugitive from a Georgia chain gang, but not by much."

"Last night I talked to three of her friends. Nobody has any idea where she's gotten to."

"Could they be covering for her?"

"Possible, but it didn't sound like anyone was lying to me," I said. "I did a lot of interviewing back in my *LA Times* days, and I can usually tell when somebody's hiding something."

"Remind me to take you on my next scavenger hunt."

"And this morning I called Joel Farber out at Warlock. Told him we'd decided to investigate Spellman's murder," I informed Groucho. "So what we ought to do now is get out to the studio and start looking around."

"If Dorothy left a trail of crumbs, it would be a big help," he said. "Not only could we locate her, but we could save on lunch. Especially if they're bagel crumbs or—"

The phone on his desk rang. "If it's a creditor," Groucho said into the receiver, "I'm on an extended tour of Central America. If it's a Central American creditor, simply say I've flown the coop. You might add, Nanette, that I hold the world's record for solo coop flying and have a large trophy to . . . oh, so? Put her on." He handed me the phone. "It's Jane, but you needn't fret. Has nothing to do with your impending offspring."

"Hi, what's up?"

Jane said, "I've got a feeling I'd better not go into too many details over the phone."

"That's accepted B-movie detective logic."

"Enery just phoned," explained my wife. "He'd very much like you to meet him, soon as you can, at a cottage in Westwood." She gave me the address, which was over near the UCLA campus.

"Is Groucho invited, too?" I asked.

"He wasn't specifically excluded, so, if you must, I suppose you can drag him along."

"This has to do with what we were about talking about last night?"

"Yep. He's got some information in the missing persons area."

"Okay, ma'am, we'll get right over there," I told her. "How are you feeling?"

"You know how pregnant women have cravings for strange things?"

"I do, yeah."

"Well, for the past couple hours I've had a craving for Warner Baxter."

"It'll pass," I assured her. "Bye, sweetheart."

Groucho sighed soulfully as I hung up. "Ah, young love," he said, rolling his eyes.

"Surely you can still recall when you were young and in love."

"Yes, it occurred while I was charging up San Juan Hill with Teddy Roosevelt."

"Would you like to accompany me to Westwood to talk to Enery McBride?"

"Has the lad unearthed something?"

I said, "I have a hunch he knows where Dorothy Woodrow is."

Six

Groucho parked his Cadillac on a side street off Westwood Boulevard. He'd been telling me what Nan had to say about Randy Spellman's private life. "The lad's past ought to be delved into," he concluded, easing out of the car.

"I'll handle that," I volunteered.

The afternoon was bright and clear. A warm, gentle wind was drifting through the pepper trees lining the narrow lane we were walking along.

We'd covered less than a block when, from a large, ramshackle white house up ahead on our right, a bunch of college kids emerged. Two girls and three guys, the huskiest guy wearing a blue-and-gold UCLA letterman sweater.

He was the first one to recognize Groucho. Stopping on the sidewalk about ten feet in front of us, he cried out, "Hey, Groucho, have you shot any elephants in your pajamas lately?"

Shuffling to a stop, Groucho eyed him. "Of late, young sir, I've been limiting myself to shooting down louts who quote lines from my old movies."

A pretty blonde in a plaid skirt, white sweater, and saddle

shoes asked, "When are you going to do another radio show, Mr. Marx?"

"My colleague Mr. Denby," he said, gesturing in my direction, "and I have a terrific, I might even describe it as supercolossal, radio program in the works. It's entitled *Dead Air with Groucho Marx* and consists of nothing but complete silence for thirty minutes."

"Thus far, though," I added, "Groucho's been unable to remain silent for more than a minute and a half, which is hindering our attempts to sell the show to a network."

"Aren't you," inquired the other coed, a plump redhead, "the fellow who writes the *Hollywood Molly* radio show?"

"I am, yeah."

"I think that's a very funny program. We listen to it in the dorm every—"

"Ahum," observed Groucho, and consulted his watch. "If this conversation isn't going to stay concentrated on me, I suggest—"

"Seriously, Mr. Marx, when are you going to do another radio show?" asked the blonde, shifting her grip on three hefty textbooks.

"Seriously, I'm going to be replacing President Roosevelt on his Fireside Chat broadcasts," he replied. "FDR's been getting extremely sooty on his left side from sitting so close to the fireplace, and he's taking a hiatus. Originally he was going to take a Greyhound bus, but the Secret Service felt—"

"We'd best be continuing on our way," I cut in to suggest.

"Pity I forgot to bring my guitar."

"One man's pity is—"

"Farewell to all and sundry. And especially to you, Our Girl Sundry." He grasped the blonde coed's hand and kissed it enthusiastically. "I regret not being able to kiss both your mitts.

However, if you make an appointment with my social secretary, I should be able to handle it before the year is out."

As we moved on, one of the college boys observed, "Groucho's still pretty spry for an old man."

"You've used that Our Girl Sundry line before," I mentioned.

"True, but we old men get very sentimental about our favorite bons mots."

The address Enery had passed along was at the end of the block. It was a Tudor-style cottage, overly quaint, and fronted by a yard full of flowers and shrubs.

Sprawled in a lopsided wicker armchair on the stone porch was a weatherworn ventriloquist's dummy. He had on a tattered tuxedo, was missing one shoe and his left eye. All in all, he looked very forlorn slumped there in the midday sunlight.

Contemplating the dummy, Groucho said, "I'd heard that Charlie McCarthy had been hitting the sauce. But I didn't realize he'd fallen so low."

I knocked, quietly, on the door.

The door, quietly, opened about three inches. "Hi, Frank. Hello, Mr. Marx."

"Jane said you had something to tell us," I mentioned.

"C'mon in," Enery invited. "Dorothy can tell you herself."

The ventriloquist dummies that shared the cottage parlor with us were in much better shape than the fellow on the porch. The dummy inhabiting one side of the candy-striped love seat was a golden-haired moppet in a gingham dress, the one sharing the sofa with me was a freckled kid of twelve, and the dummy straddling the arm of Groucho's Morris chair was a plump old gent with a walrus moustache and a military air.

"This cottage belongs to a friend of Dorothy's, fellow named Arnie Carr." Enery was standing in the doorway. "The guy is, as you maybe guessed, a ventriloquist. Right now he's up in the town of Santa Francesca for their Fiesta Week, doing his act at a local inn."

I asked him, "Has Dorothy been here since she disappeared?"

"Yeah, she has. She's known him for years and has a spare key."

"Why," inquired Groucho, "is she hiding out at all?"

"She'll explain that."

Dorothy made her entrance then. She was wearing dark slacks and a light blue pullover. Her blonde hair was pulled back, her face pale, and her eyes were underscored with shadows. She walked with a slight limp. "Hello, Frank. Hello, Mr. Marx."

Enery took her arm, helped her settle into a fat orange armchair. He slid a fat orange ottoman under her left leg. "I know we can trust you guys," he said.

"You can," I assured him.

"I didn't kill Randy Spellman," Dorothy told us. "Fact is, he was dead when I got there."

"I figured as much," I said. "But—"

"Why were you there?" Groucho asked.

She sighed, leaning forward and rubbing at her left knee. "Because I was set up. At least it sure as hell looks like I was."

"Give them the details," Enery urged.

"As most everybody knows, including the cops and the newspapers, I had . . . well, I guess you could call it a fling with Randy. It didn't take me long to realize what a bastard he was," said Dorothy. "Problem was, Randy could be very nasty if you called things off before he was ready to move on to another dame."

Enery was sitting on a footstool near her. "Tell them about the pictures."

"Randy took some pictures of me. You could call them embarrassing," the stuntwoman continued. "After I broke off with him, Randy threatened to show them around. He wasn't in them." She leaned, took a cigarette out of the box atop the claw-footed coffee table. Enery lit it for her. "After a while, he didn't mention the pictures, quit making threats."

Wrinkling her nose, she snuffed the cigarette out in a yellow ceramic ashtray. "When I started working on this new Ty-Gor movie, Randy brought up the pictures again," Dorothy said. "He promised to give them to me, negatives and prints, if . . . if I'd do him certain favors."

"Told you he was a son of a bitch," Enery said to me.

Sighing again, Dorothy said, "Two days ago I got a note from Randy. At least, I thought it was from him. He explained that he realized what a rat he'd been and that he had decided to give the pictures to me with no strings. I was to meet the guy in his dressing room at seven o'clock that night. Even though I still didn't trust him, I figured it was worth a try."

I asked, "You still have the note?"

"Nope, I tossed it in a garbage bin on the lot."

"Handwritten?" asked Groucho.

"Typed."

"Speaking of notes," Groucho said, "what about the threatening one from you that the police found in Spellman's trailer?"

She spread her hands wide. "I didn't write him any damned notes, Mr. Marx."

"What happened when you got to his dressing room that night?"

"Randy was already dead. He was sprawled out on his back in front of his trailer."

I asked, "Did you see or hear anything?"

"There was an odd perfume in the air," she answered. "I could smell it above the odor of gunpowder. Something like sandalwood, but not exactly."

"Know anybody who wears a perfume like that?"

She shook her head. "No, Frank."

"Anything else?"

Dorothy hesitated, finally replying, "I'm not sure."

"She thought somebody might be watching her from off in the jungle," said Enery, putting his hand on hers. "In the shadows, but she's not sure."

"It did cross my mind that whoever killed Randy might still be hanging around," Dorothy said. "And I also was pretty damn sure somebody was trying to get me mixed up in his murder. So I got out of there."

"You didn't think about calling the police?"

"No," she said, shaking her head. "I didn't want anybody to know I'd been anywhere near the guy that night. I didn't know about that fake note, but I did know Randy had been telling a lot of people that I was still carrying the torch for him."

"She was afraid," added Enery, "that the police might jump to exactly the wrong conclusions they *have* jumped to."

"I wasn't even sure that I wanted to get Enery involved," Dorothy said. "But I finally decided to call him." She smiled at the actor.

Groucho asked her, "How'd you get out of the Warlock studio grounds?"

"Climbed over the back wall," she replied, rubbing at her knee again. "Not too tough to do, except I took a spill when I landed outside."

Enery asked me, "Can you help her?"

"We can try to find out who really killed Spellman," I answered. "But she ought to come out of hiding, get a good lawyer, and then get in touch with the police."

"Not yet," said Dorothy. "I'm just not ready to—"

"Longer you wait," I told her, "the guiltier you're going to look."

"I know, yes, but . . ."

Groucho stood up. "Who do you think might've killed Spellman?"

"I don't know," she said. "But a hell of a lot of people must be happy that he's dead and gone."

Seven

The morning was gray, and by the time I reached Studio City at around 10 A.M., a misty drizzle had commenced. I turned off Laurel Canyon Boulevard onto Woodbridge and found a parking place just about across the street from the Stardust Diner.

The diner represented an architect's idea of what a streamlined railroad dining car might look like, possibly one that both Buck Rogers and Flash Gordon patronized. It was sleek and silver on the outside, generously trimmed with swirling neon tubing in bright basic colors.

As I reached out to push the bright blue door, it was pushed open from inside. Chester Morris, looking dapper as usual, was coming out.

"Hi, kid," he said. "Are you a father yet?"

"Couple weeks more."

"Jane doing okay?"

"Fine thus far."

The actor said, "Give the lady my best. And think about writing a movie for me sometime." Turning up his coat color and readjusting his snap-brim hat, he hurried away into the fuzzy gray morning.

For some reason that was not immediately discernible, all the waitresses were wearing sombreros. I spotted my friend from the Studio City police force sitting at a silvery booth midway back.

"It's Mexican Specials Day," explained Detective Mitch Tandofsky as I sat down opposite him in the glittering streamlined booth.

"Hence the sombreros."

"You ought to drop in on Alaska Fish Specials Day." Resting next to his coffee mug was a new brown-leather briefcase. "Two reasons why I agreed to talk to you about the Spellman murder, Frank." Mitch was a slightly overweight man in his middle thirties, a bit on the short side and with a bald spot starting to break through his tight-curling black hair. "First off, we've been buddies since the days when you earned an honest living with the *LA Times*. Secondly," he added, lowering his raspy voice, "I don't happen to agree with some of my colleagues."

"About who actually killed Spellman?"

"Exactly, right. I happen to know Dorothy Woodrow. Used to date her. That was, oh, two, three years ago," the detective said. "I don't believe she could've killed the guy. Therefore, I am not buying the notion that she fled to avoid getting arrested." He drank some of his coffee. "Besides, it looks to me like a whole stewpot of people had reasons for killing him."

"That's what, so far, Groucho and I think." I didn't mention that Dorothy herself shared our belief.

"Okay, Frank, I brought—"

"Can I interest you boys in a Mexican Special?" asked the pretty blonde waitress who'd materialized beside our booth and was tipping her sombrero by way of greeting.

"Not at this hour," I replied. "Just coffee for now."

"And a refill for me, Barbara," said Tandofsky.

"I'm thinking, Mitch, of changing my name."

"Barbara's a fine name."

"Sure, but Googins isn't. Not for a marquee," explained the pretty waitress. "Barbara Googins in *Drums Along the Mohawk,* Barbara Googins in *The Mark of Zorro.* No oomph."

"Heck of a lot more oomph than Tandofsky," he assured her. "Anyway, I wouldn't change it until I got a studio contract, Barbara. Then let them think up a new one for you."

"That may be a long time from now." She smiled, somewhat forlornly, and departed.

"What about the alleged threatening note?" I asked.

Unzipping the briefcase, he reached inside. He brought out a photo of the letter that had been found in the murdered man's dressing room, handed it to me.

It was typed, meaning anybody could've written the thing. I said as much, then asked, "Whose fingerprints are on it?"

Mitch narrowed one eye. "Nobody's."

"How's that? Dorothy supposedly sent it to him, he supposedly read it," I pointed out. "How'd they do that without anyone touching it?"

"That's sure what they call an anomaly," said Mitch, leaning back on his bench. "My colleagues can't explain it, but they've still got Dorothy at the head of their suspect list. We got copies of both Dorothy and Spellman's prints from their studio personnel files."

"Can I keep this copy?"

"Go ahead. Show it to Groucho."

Folding the photo in half, I tucked it into the breast pocket of my jacket. "Were Dorothy's fingerprints anywhere in the dressing room?"

"Nope, but she could've been wearing gloves."

"Who are your other suspects?"

"So far I've got a list of quite a few people who won't mourn Spellman," my friend answered. "I wouldn't say they were all exactly suspects. At the moment, I'm not going to share that information with you, Frank."

Barbara Googins brought us two cups of coffee. "If you change your minds and want a Breakfast Tamale, let me know."

"We hear," I said, "that besides fooling around with a wide range of women, I said that Spellman might also have dabbled in blackmail now and then."

"I've heard that, too."

"And specific targets?"

"That's more stuff I'm not up to sharing just yet."

I sampled my coffee. "Suppose something's happened to Dorothy as well?"

"That's a possibility, Frank, and we're looking into it."

"If she's hiding for some reason and comes out into the open," I asked, "what would happen then?"

"At the very least, she'd be held for questioning," Tandofsky said. "And she might even be charged with murder. All depends. But maybe I can find the real killer before that happens."

"Or maybe Groucho and I will find the killer."

Mitch nodded, smiling briefly. "Stranger things have happened," he admitted.

The windshield wipers on Groucho's Cadillac were wiping in waltz time, or so he later told me, as he halted at the gates of the Warlock studios. The drizzle was in the act of converting into rain.

A guard, whose uniform fit him perfectly, except around the middle, leaned out of his hut to inquire, "Yeah?"

Rolling his window down halfway, Groucho informed him, "I have an appointment with Joel Farber."

"And who might you be?"

"Well, if I had a choice, I might be the elusive Scarlet Pimpernel or, better yet, the sixth Dione Quintuplet," he replied. "But, alas, I'm stuck with being a poor, but honest, country lad named Groucho Marx."

After making a grunting noise, the guard reached into his hut for a clipboard. Consulting the mimeographed list attached, he said, "Says here you're an actor."

"Remind me to sue somebody for slander," he said. "I take it you've never seen me upon the silver screen? Or even the kitchen screen?"

"I never go to the movies," the guard confided, making a check beside Groucho's name. "I spend my leisure time reading great books. I belong to a reading club."

"I couldn't afford the fee for the great books club and had to settle for the trashy fiction club."

"Drive on in and park in Lot 3." The guard ducked back into his hut.

The iron gates swung open inward, silently, and Groucho guided his rain-spattered car onto the lot.

Tall palm trees rose up on each side of the entrance to the visitors' lot. Gathered under one of them for partial shelter were three cattle rustlers and two dance-hall girls. The red-haired dancer was holding a folded copy of the *LA Times* over her head, and the meanest-looking cattle rustler was attempting to roll a cigarette.

Groucho parked next to a silver Jaguar. "Ah, it must be pleasant to listen to rain go pitter-patter on a Jaguar roof." He got out of the car, headed for the street.

"Hello, Groucho," called the rustler, who was still trying to concoct a cigarette.

"Howdy," Groucho said. "You ought to switch to cigars. Although, admittedly, they're even tougher to roll."

"Don't you have an umbrella, Groucho?" asked the redhead.

He paused, patted himself, and then answered, "Apparently not."

"Like part of my newspaper?"

"Only if I can have the pages with the funnies. Lately I've become obsessed with the peregrinations of Little Orphan Annie."

The dance-hall girl separated off a section of the *Times,* handed it to him.

Unfurling it, Groucho held it over his head. "I'll be eternally grateful, ma'm," he assured her, "well into next week."

The blonde dance-hall girl asked, "Are you really going to investigate that rat's murder?"

"Be more specific, my child. Which rat?"

Her nose wrinkled. "I mean Randy Spellman," she said. "Seems to me, now that he's dead and gone, you should just forget about it."

Groucho said, "If we did that, we wouldn't be able to prove that Dorothy Woodrow didn't do him in."

A bearded cattle rustler said, "Dorothy didn't kill Spellman."

"Oh, so? Can you tell us who did, in twenty-five words or less?"

When the bit player shook his head, raindrops that had collected on his Stetson splattered the front of Groucho's plaid sports coat. "Nope, it's just that I know Dorothy," he said, "and she's not the sort of girl to kill anybody."

The blonde suggested, "Maybe it was old Arthur Wright Benson himself. I hear he didn't think Randy was right for Ty-Gor anymore."

The other dance-hall girl said, "I worked on the last Ty-Gor—I was one of the Amazons. We shot a lot of that one out at Benson's estate, and the word was that Randy was way too friendly with old Benson's new wife."

"You can't narrow it down to the Benson clan," said the rustler as he finally completed making the cigarette and stuffed the sack of tobacco back into his shirt pocket. "Most everybody who ever worked with Randy disliked the guy."

Tipping his newspaper, Groucho said, "Thank you one and all. And now I must be going."

Knees slightly bent, he went loping off in the direction of Joel Farber's office.

Eight

Somebody had taped a slightly bedraggled black wreath to the metal door of Soundstage 3.

"What half-wit did that?" muttered Joel Farber as he opened the door.

"Apparently Spellman has at least one mourner," observed Groucho, following the producer into the huge, shadowy building.

"Maybe it's meant ironically."

"A movie lot's an odd place to encounter irony."

The overhead lights in the vicinity of Randy Spellman's trailer and the spurious jungle were on. Where the body had been sprawled in the floor, there was now a chalk outline of the jungle man.

In a canvas director's chair a few yards from the trailer sat a uniformed studio guard, legs crossed, reading a tattered copy of *Ranch Romances.* "Nothing's happening, Mr. Farber," he announced, closing the pulp magazine and popping to his feet.

"Darn," said Groucho, "I was so hoping the killer'd return to the scene of the crime. That'd make everything so much easier for us all."

The young producer said, "You can take a break, Josh. Be back in fifteen."

"Thanks, Mr. Farber." Dropping his reading material on the canvas chair, the guard walked away into the shadows.

Groucho was gazing toward two rows of ten palm trees that were lined up on the far side of Spellman's portable dressing room. "Why," he inquired, gesturing with his unlit cigar, "are all those extra palm trees lurking over there in redwood tubs? They ought to be in yonder jungle."

Joel Farber halted on the first step leading up to Randy Spellman's trailer. "They would've been if Randy hadn't gotten himself bumped off," he explained. "Arthur Wright Benson thought our jungle here on the set looked a mite tacky, so he uprooted some stuff from his private jungle and sent it over. It was delivered the day of the murder."

Strolling over to the trees, which were resting in dirt and a scattering of pine chips, Groucho asked, "Benson deliver them himself?"

"No, they came in a truck from the famous Rancho Tygoro." He climbed the steps.

"How much control does Benson have over your Ty-Gor movies?"

"According to his contract, not that much." Farber was opening the door of the late king of the jungle's dressing room. "But the studio heads are inclined to pay attention to the old boy. The Ty-Gor movies do pretty damn well at the box office."

Groucho followed the producer into the trailer. "Could Benson have forced the Warlock Studios to dump Spellman?"

"It's possible, Groucho. Lately Benson had been complaining about Randy, and, let's face it, Randy was pretty replaceable."

The dressing room was large, its walls and ceiling buff-colored.

"Law me," Groucho observed, "this is twice as big as the dressing room MGM provides *me*. And it's not cluttered up with a lot of unsightly urinals the way mine is."

There were signs that a police crew had been through the place. They'd searched drawers and cabinets, dusted for fingerprints. A spent flashbulb was lying on the mat carpeting just short of a wicker wastebasket. The only picture was a framed glossy of a grinning Randy Spellman standing on the deck of a sailboat.

Hands behind his back, softly humming "Lydia the Tattooed Lady," Groucho started wandering around the room. Slightly slouched, he sniffed at the air.

Faint traces of gunpowder and that not-quite-sandalwood scent Dorothy had mentioned.

Straightening, Groucho inquired of the producer, "Is that perfume familiar to you?"

Farber said, "What perfume? I don't smell a damned thing." His brow wrinkled. "Would it be a clue?"

"Only if you could smell it."

"You're kidding, right?"

Groucho bowed his head for a few seconds. "Alas, yes, that's one of my few failings," he admitted. "That and my penchant for pastrami. And that's one of the good things about MGM—they have a dandy penchant plan. Thirty dollars every Thursday and on Friday ten pokes with a sharp—"

"I'm a bit late," I announced as I climbed into the trailer. "Got tied up in traffic."

"I once got tied up by a Scandinavian aviatrix," mentioned Groucho. "Tying middle-aged, mangy lovers up with sturdy ropes aroused a—"

"How's Jane doing, Frank?" Joel was straddling the straight-back chair in front of Spellman's makeup table.

"She's considerably calmer than I am," I replied.

Groucho asked, "Where was the alleged threatening note found?"

The producer stood, indicating the makeup mirror with a pointing thumb. "Tucked into the frame of Randy's mirror."

Crossing the room, Groucho stood looking into the mirror. "Now I understand why my wife keeps all the mirrors in our home covered with cheesecloth." Sighing moderately, he squatted and ran his fingertips over the floor. "A scattering of those pine chips from the potted palms ended up under here."

"Is that a clue?" asked Joel.

"It might be," admitted Groucho, "or it might not."

"With the cops and all sorts of studio people trooping in and out," said Joel, "just about anybody could've tracked those chips in."

"I was going to toss in a droll remark about *Good-bye, Mr. Chips,*" admitted Groucho as he straightened up. "But I've decided to refrain."

"A wise decision," I said. "By the way, the police didn't find any prints on that note."

Groucho's eyebrows climbed. "Not Dorothy Woodrow's?"

"Not hers, not Randy's."

"How do they account for that interesting state of affairs?"

"They don't. At least not for general consumption," I answered. "Fact is, they didn't find a single print of Dorothy's in this joint."

"Not that I think the poor kid's guilty of anything," put in my producer, "but she might've worn gloves, you know."

"And sent Spellman a pair to use while he read her missive," added Groucho.

Joel glanced at his gold wristwatch. "Shit, I'm late for a meeting. We have to decide who's going to replace poor Randy in this goddamn film." He moved to the doorway. "You boys can nose around all you want."

"We shall," Groucho assured him.

"And let me know as soon as you find out anything important."

"Have the police," I asked him, "told you how their investigation is coming along?"

"Nope, but who needs cops when we've got you guys?" Grinning, he hurried down the metal steps and away.

Nine

Groucho tilted back in the straight-back chair, unwrapped a fresh stogie, and held it like a conductor's baton for a few seconds. Inserting it between his teeth and not bothering to light it, he said, "Young Farber's going to be disappointed. He's expecting a flock of clues."

"Keep in mind that he hired *us*," I reminded. "Which seems to indicate that he's easily pleased."

"No need to be self-deprecating, Rollo," he told me. "Or self-defecating, for that matter. But that latter I leave up to you." He took a puff of his unlit cigar. "In my younger days I would now have fashioned a pithy remark making use of the similarity between *latter* and *ladder.*"

"Just as well."

Groucho said, "Back to business. From what you've informed me about your recent rendezvous with your flatfoot chum, the police are going to have a hard time pinning the crime on Dorothy. Unless they can come up with an explanation of how the telltale note exchanged hands without anybody touching it."

"Detective Tandofsky doesn't believe she's guilty, but some of his colleagues do. And it's possible they know more than we do."

"Highly possible."

"Turns out even Tandofsky dated Dorothy. That was a couple years back."

Groucho rose up out of the makeup table chair. "Not every woman is as steadfast as your missus." He returned the naked cigar to his coat pocket. "Something not quite perfume lingers in the air, pine chips are scattered on the floor where the fake missive was planted and no place else." Shaking his head, he went slouching toward the door. "Did the minions of the law unearth any of Spellman's blackmail paraphernalia?"

"There are a lot of facts Tandofsky isn't sharing with me." I followed him down the stairs. "By now they've also gone through Spellman's place in Malibu. But it's unlikely I'll be able to learn what they've dug up."

"Well, right now we'll simply have to cast our bread upon the waters," he said, heading in the direction of the indoor jungle. "And with any luck, within a few days we'll have a whole lot of soggy bread."

"I'm going to see my friend May Sankowitz this afternoon."

"The estimable lady who's employed at *Hollywood Screen* magazine and is a veritable fount of Hollywood gossip and scandal?"

"That May Sankowitz, yeah."

Groucho halted near a stand of tall palm trees from which dangled very believable-looking vines. "Whilst you're gathering background on Spellman's lives and loves, young sir, I'll be dropping by the Hillcrest Country Club," he informed me. "As you may recall, the Hillcrest is the only country club in all of Greater Los Angeles that will accept Talmudic scholars such as myself as members. I intend to have an informative chat with Lew Hershman."

"Spellman's agent, that's a good idea."

"Spellman's agent *and* a bondified goniff. Just the chap to inform me about the skeletons in Spellman's closet and provide a thorough enemy list."

"But it's raining, so he can't play golf. You sure the guy will be there?"

"Hershman has never laid a hand on a golf club, Rollo. He goes to the Hillcrest most afternoons to play pinochle."

"I'll telephone you tonight, Groucho. We can compare notes and plan our next moves."

"Since you're close to Enery McBride, try to get him to persuade Dorothy to turn herself in." Eyes narrowing, Groucho lurched forward.

Working his way through some bright green imitation brush, he leaned toward a patch of real ferns. "Here's an interesting bit of ephemera," he mentioned as he plucked a small lace-trimmed handkerchief that was entangled with a fern. "Smells a bit like sandalwood."

Emerging from the foliage, he held the hanky near my nose. "That it does," I agreed.

"In all the Agatha Christie mystery novels I've ever read—which amounts to one and a half—a handkerchief always has telltale initials embroidered on it. Say "GM," for instance, and that leads the amateur sleuth to suspect that the killer is Gustav Mahler or George Murphy or Gene Markey or—though I have an ironclad and slightly rusty alibi—Groucho Marx."

"No initials on this one, though."

"If I were given to profanity, I'd say, 'Drat it all,' at this point." He folded the hanky and slipped it into a jacket side pocket that he didn't store cigars in. "No initials, no laundry marks, no spots of blood."

"Dorothy had the feeling somebody was still hanging around that night," I said, nodding toward the jungle. "It could've been a woman."

"It could well have been a woman lurking. *Lurking* is, I believe, the apter word." Knees slightly bent, he made his way across the darkened soundstage toward the exit. "I was quite good at lurking in my youth, but then I graduated to peeping. You've no doubt heard the expression 'The man's a regular Peeping Groucho.'"

"Possibly once."

"Yes, it's not catching on the way we planned."

Outside, the rain was coming down heavier.

Heading away from the Warlock studios, I clicked on the radio in my Chevy. As fate would have it, I came in on the middle of one of Johnny Whistler's Hollywood gossip broadcasts.

". . . have an open letter to Tyrone Power," the columnist was saying in his piping voice. "But first a bit of good advice to that over-the-hill movie clown, Julius 'Groucho' Marx. Groucho, you're a movie actor and not a detective. Forget the brutal murder of the late, gifted Randy Spellman, whom all of moviedom is mourning, and leave the investigation to those who are qualified for such serious work. Admittedly, you've had a bit of luck in the past, sticking your nose into other people's murder business. But, take it from me, enough is enough. And stop leading that screenwriter stooge of yours astray. His lovely and enormously gifted wife is Jane Danner, who draws the marvelous comic strip *Hollywood Molly* in the *Los Angeles Times,* which is one of the more than seven hundred newspapers that carry my column. She's expecting a visit from Brother Stork any edition now, and her hubby should be at her side and not aiding and abetting you in your follies. So, take a . . ."

I switched stations and got a cooking show. A kindly old lady told me how to fry my lamb chops in lard.

Jane listened to Whistler quite a bit in order to keep up with Hollywood news. If she'd heard Whistler's diatribe, it probably had upset her. I decided to stop by home before catching up with May Sankowitz.

Myra Kendig was a twenty-year-old art school grad. A blonde, she was somewhere between slender and skinny, and she'd been assisting Jane on her comic strip since the previous December.

When I stopped home that rainy afternoon, Myra and Dorgan were in the studio. She was at Jane's drawing board, filling in backgrounds on a *Hollywood Molly* daily.

Dorgan was sprawled near her feet and snoring with considerable vigor.

"Hi, Mr. Denby." She smiled. "Jane's resting."

"Did she happen to hear—"

"Johnny Whistler? Oh, yes, she did," Myra answered. "We never did get to hear that jerk's open letter to Tyrone Power."

"Did Jane throw the portable radio or simply turn it off?"

"Started to toss it, thought better, and clicked the darn thing off."

"Good, in her condition she shouldn't be throwing radios around. Even small ones."

Wide awake, Dorgan was staring up at me. He decided he knew me and proceeded to stand up on his hind legs and lick my hand.

"You know, Mr. Denby," said Myra as she set her pen on the taboret, "Jane's not anywhere as delicate as you think."

"I'm aware of that," I acknowledged. "Thing is, Myra, I've had no previous experience of impending fatherhood, and so—"

"Why aren't you out sleuthing?" Jane appeared in the doorway, fresh from her nap.

I went to her, took her hand. "Made a stop en route," I explained. "Happened to hear Whistler's show, and I thought you—"

"No, he didn't upset me," my wife assured me. "Although, that part about your being a stooge did seem to ring true, don't you think?"

Dorgan trotted over, looked up at her, and attempted to smile and pant at the same time.

"You sure you're okay, Jane?"

"Fit as a fiddle, tip-top, crackerjack, and so forth. Really," she said, kissing me on the cheek. "Takes more than that pipsqueak to unsettle me."

"Actually, I may've used that half-wit broadcast as an excuse to stop by and see you," I admitted as we went into the living room.

"As I interpret the California marriage laws, you can visit me as often as you care to without needing any excuse at all."

"No kidding? Is that something those pesky Socialists snuck through?"

Jane sat on the sofa. "How are you and Groucho coming along?"

Sitting beside her, holding her hand, I gave her a condensed version of what we'd dug up thus far. I didn't have to do all that much condensing, since we hadn't as yet gathered a mass of information.

I ended up with, "If Enery telephones, urge the guy to get Dorothy to quit being a fugitive, huh?"

"I will, yes."

I stood up. "I've got an appointment to talk to May Sankowitz."

"I'm not a bit jealous," she told me.

Ten

Groucho decided to stop at his office for a change of sports coats and a new supply of cigars before venturing on to the Hillcrest Country Club. He also wanted to lock the perfumed handkerchief away in a desk drawer.

Standing near the entrance to the building was a dark-haired young man wearing a loose-fitting brown suit and a bold blue-and-orange hand-painted necktie. "Excuse me, sir," he said timidly.

"I can excuse everything but that necktie."

"I understand that Groucho Marx has an office somewhere in this building here."

"Do you happen to be a process server, a bill collector, or a disgruntled husband?"

"No, sir, I'm a tourist from Iola, Wisconsin, and I was hoping to get his autograph."

"Groucho Marx," murmured Groucho thoughtfully. "Groucho Marx. The name does ring a bell. Or rather it rings a distant gong. He's that singing cowboy, is he not?"

"No, sir, Groucho Marx is a funny comedian. You know, part of the Marx Brothers."

"Which part? Never mind, don't tell me. I can guess," he said. "What exactly does this low buffoon look like?"

The young man, fiddling with his gaudy tie, had been studying Groucho's face. "Well, he sort of looks like you. Except he's got a moustache and he wears baggy pants, a badly fitting coat, and he makes rude remarks all the time."

"Then except for the moustache I could well be he."

"Gee, are you?" He produced a thick autograph book from inside his jacket.

Groucho accepted the album. "In point of fact, I'm the world's greatest forger, and I can produce a Groucho Marx autograph that will fool them back in Racine, Wisconsin."

"Iola, Wisconsin."

"There, too." He signed the book with one of his own fountain pens, returned the book to the partially stunned fan, and went bounding gracefully up the stairs to his second-floor office.

Nan looked up from her typing. "Your fame as a detective is spreading."

"So's that rash on my backside," Groucho said. "Truth to tell, I dare not sit down for fear of—"

"You've had two phone calls from a lady who sounds most eager to talk to you about Randy Spellman."

Perching on the edge of his secretary's desk, he inquired, "Who?"

"None other than Laura Dayton."

"Columbia Pictures' answer to Bette Davis," he said. "And, until a couple years ago, Randy Spellman's spouse."

"She divorced the guy at least *three* years ago," said Nan. "But she says she's got some interesting stuff she'd rather tell you than the cops."

"Where and when would she like to tell all?"

"She wants to know if you can drop by her place in Bel Air around six tonight."

"I can."

"Then I'll phone her," said Nan. "She bought, you know, the Barney Kains mansion a while back."

Groucho sighed. "Kains was an admirable silent comedian. He used to be a very funny man."

"So did you," said Nan.

I decided to wait under the long, wide awning in front of Earl Carroll's restaurant and nightspot on Sunset for May Sankowitz. Tucked under my arm was a furled red-and-yellow-polka-dot umbrella Jane had loaned me.

May was inside, due out shortly, attending the Golden Orange Award luncheon. Once a year in the spring, the members of the Motion Picture Reporters and Columnists League passed out a bunch of awards to movie people.

Not feeling up to watching the tail end of the festivities, I was stationed on the sidewalk. Across the boulevard I noticed somebody that I was pretty sure was Edgar Bergen heading toward the CBS building. Built in a style that was a movie art director's notion of Art Deco, the Columbia Broadcasting complex was a fairly new addition to Sunset. Bergen was carrying a paper shopping bag, but it didn't look roomy enough to tote Charlie McCarthy around in.

"Hi, Frank. How's Jane getting along?"

Joan Blondell had just stepped out of Earl Carroll's, and a gray Packard was pulling up to the curb for her.

"Much better than I am."

The blonde actress asked, "Isn't your baby about due?"

"Less than three weeks."

"Say hello to Jane for me," she instructed me as she stepped into the backseat of the car. "Oh, and don't worry about Whistler calling you a stooge."

The door closed, the Packard drove away into the afternoon rain.

"You could've come inside to wait, Frank." May Sankowitz had emerged and was taking hold of my arm.

"Say, Frank, you really aren't a stooge for Groucho." Joe E. Brown was following in May's wake, clutching a baseball-sized gold orange to his chest. "Most Lovable Movie Comedian again this year. Box-office poison, but still lovable." He grinned his very wide grin and went jogging toward the parking lot.

May asked, "Have I mentioned to you that I've become a vegetarian?"

"At least twice, yeah."

She was a small, compact woman of about fifty. Her short-cropped hair was an autumn-leaf brown at the moment. "Since I am, I didn't eat much lunch in there. Let's go someplace where you can treat me to a nutburger."

"Can we get to such a place without crossing state lines?"

She nudged me in the side with an elbow. "Little joint called the Garden Spot is just around the corner. We can walk there."

I unfurled the umbrella, held it high, and we started off.

The Garden Spot was just wide enough to squeeze two rows of six white-covered tables into. It smelled of raw fruit, steamed vegetables, and herbs.

Our waiter was suntanned and muscular, and sometime in

the recent past he'd had a nose job. He showed us to one of the several empty tables and took May's order for a nutburger on Russian rye and mine for a glass of mango-papaya juice.

Resting both elbows on the tabletop, May said, "I'll provide you with some background info on Spellman. In return, Frank dear, I'd appreciate it if you'd pass along to me whatever little tidbits you and Groucho gather. You know, stuff I can use on my nightly broadcast or in my column or even in the magazine."

"Sure, I'll—"

"Also, telephone me as soon as Jane has the baby," my friend added. "Unlike you, she's getting to be a celebrity. And try to get the news to me in time for one of my radio shows."

"I'll urge Jane to be prompt. Now about—"

"You working for Enery McBride?"

"Eh?" I said, cupping my ear.

"He's a good buddy of you and Jane, he's been Dorothy Woodrow's lover for the past few months. So I figure you—"

"We're trying to help him. But how'd you know about him and—"

"Finding out such stuff is my calling in life, remember?" she reminded.

The waiter brought her sandwich and my juice.

Taking an enthusiastic bite of her nutburger, May chewed for a moment and then asked, "How well do you know Dorothy?"

"Not well, know her from running into her at the studios now and then."

"Enery's not in for a long-term romance."

"Meaning?"

She took another bite, shrugging one shoulder. "She's a restless young lady," she answered. "For a while it was Randy Spellman,

69

then there were a couple of others, then it was Enery's turn. No way to tell who'll be next."

"Whether she's restless or not, Enery is convinced that she had nothing to do with the murder and that she was framed."

"Hey, I don't think she killed that bastard," said May, taking a sip of her glass of mineral water. "She's not the kind of dame to get that serious—serious enough to kill somebody—over any guy."

"Suppose he was blackmailing her? That'd give her a motive."

May shook her head. "Naw, not Dorothy Woodrow," she persisted.

"He was a blackmailer, though. Do you know some of his targets?"

"I have a list of about a half dozen of his victims that I'm certain about back at my office. I'll have one of my assistants type you a copy, Frank, and messenger it over to your place."

"Anybody else who wanted to do him harm?"

"If I was digging into this mess, I'd take a good, long look at the Arthur Wright Benson family."

"AWB himself?"

"Let me explain." She finished her nutburger, signaled the waiter to bring another one. "Stop me if you've heard this basic scenario before. The old boy is close to sixty-five, and his newest wife is not quite thirty. Her name was Marge Rawson, and she's been Marge Benson for two years. Before that, she was the runner-up in a Miss Montana contest and then journeyed to the Golden West to find fame, fortune, or a rich sugar daddy. Since she has good looks but not a speck of talent, it was lucky for her that Benson stumbled upon her at a party on one of his cronies' yachts."

"A heartwarming tale. What's it got to do with Spellman?"

After beginning on the second nutburger, May continued.

"As you know, Frank dear, the previous Ty-Gor epic was shot out at Rancho Tygoro." She paused to chuckle. "Good thing that wasn't Sir Arthur Conan Doyle's spread, or it'd be named Rancho Sherlocko."

"You're leading up to Randy's having an affair with the current Mrs. Benson?"

"Bingo," May said. "Old AWB was never quite certain anything had happened, but he decided he didn't want Randy in any further Ty-Gor flickers."

"So if he later found out for sure—he'd have a nice motive for doing away with Spellman?"

"Or for hiring some goons to do the job and try to frame Dorothy, sure," she added. "As you have possibly noticed, Frank dear, Hollywood is a very superstitious town. If I believed in any of that crap, I'd say there was quite probably a jinx on Rancho Tygoro. Or maybe a hex."

"How so?"

"Well, at about the same time Randy Spellman was sneaking Marge Benson up into his tree house, Alicia Benson—the old boy's daughter—was losing her fiancée."

"How'd she do that?"

"Not exactly her fault, although she's known to turn nasty when she's in her cups," said May. "This latest beau was an accountant with Arthur Wright Benson, Inc. Named Cahan or some such, and one moonless night he decided he liked fifteen thousand dollars better than he liked fair Alicia and absconded with that sum. He's probably far, far south of the border at present."

I remembered to drink some of my juice. It tasted pretty good. "Don't forget to send me that victim list."

"And don't forget to let me know as soon as your kid is

born," May said. "Call me from the hospital. It'll make a nice folksy item for my show."

I smiled at her. "You've become pretty crass."

"I was always crass," she assured me.

Hillcrest was high up on West Pico Boulevard, and rain was falling enthusiastically on the vast green of the golf course when Groucho guided his Cadillac into the members' parking lot.

At their regular round table in the dining room, several of his pals were gathered, including George Burns, Jack Benny, Harry Ruby, and Georgie Jessel. Groucho, as he recounted to me later, paused beside the table while on his way to join Randy Spellman's agent at a small table on the far side of the big room.

"As usual," Groucho assured me, "this gathering of woebegone would-be wits tried desperately to come up with even one small clever remark. Alas, I regret to say, they failed miserably. Burns tried valiantly, but only succeeded in provoking a fit of giggles in Benny. And that's not difficult to achieve. After scattering a few pearls of wit, I went on about my business."

Lew Hershman was a sleek, graying man in his middle fifties. He wore a turquoise polo shirt and a blazer of indeterminate color. "Things are definitely looking up, Groucho."

"Ah, would that all agents took the death of a client so well, Lew." Groucho lowered himself into the seat opposite.

"Listen, I just got word that the client I been trying to sell Warlock to replace Randy as Ty-Gor is going to be hired."

"And he is?"

"Carl Nesbit. I hear old Arthur Wright Benson thinks Carl's perfect to take over as Ty-Gor." Hershman smiled. "And unlike poor Randy, this guy can speak in whole sentences."

"C'mon, Nesbit isn't an actor, he's a swimmer."

"So who needs a Barrymore to wear a jockstrap and climb trees?"

Producing a cigar, Groucho lit it. "I'm hoping it won't pain you too much to tell me a little about Randy Spellman."

"I can control my emotions," the agent told him, checking his gold wristwatch. "But let's make it snappy, because I got a pinochle game coming up in about fifteen minutes."

Eleven

Groucho heard the first scream while he was hurrying up the slippery marble steps of Laura Dayton's sprawling Bel-Air mansion.

He'd arrived at her place just off St. Cloud Road a couple moments earlier, parked near the five-car garage, and dashed across the wide white-gravel drive.

The house had been built in the 1920s and looked like an uneasy partnership between a California mission and an Arabian Nights palace. Pale blue minarets were mixed with slanting red-tile roofs, and wrought-iron grillwork decorated walls rich with exotic mosaic-tile designs. The rain had turned to a misty drizzle, and twilight seemed to be closing in early on the foliage-filled acres surrounding the imaginary palace that had once belonged to a silent-movie comic.

Sprinting up the nine steps to the carved oak door, Groucho whapped on it with his fist.

He heard another scream, this one tinged with pain. Then a shattering crash from somewhere deep inside the actress's mansion.

He knocked again, harder.

And still no one came to let him in.

Trying the big brass doorknob, he found that it turned. He pushed the door open, took a deep breath, and stepped into the house.

The long hallway had Persian carpets spread out along its length. On the stucco walls hung Eastern tapestries and brass ornaments. The whole area smelled of ancient incense.

"What ho?" shouted Groucho into the shadowy silence.

From above came a faint, hollow thump.

Feeling not a bit of fear, he later informed me, Groucho went dashing bravely up the curving staircase to the second floor.

Halfway along the hallway a door stood half-open. Inside the room someone moaned.

"I do hope that isn't a death rattle," Groucho said to himself as he edged closer.

The room turned out to be a large den, with a heavy wooden desk at its center. On the dark-paneled walls hung an impressive collection of framed publicity shots of Laura Dayton. On the Moroccan throw rug in front of the big desk, Laura herself was in the process of trying to sit up.

"Allow me." Groucho trotted over to help the dark-haired actress rise.

"Can you beat the nerve of some people?" she said. "Hiya, Groucho."

"What's befallen you?"

Upright, she grimaced and touched her fingertips to her pale forehead. "Is there a bruise?"

"I fear so. Now what exactly—"

"Could you shut that darn window?"

The large window in the far wall was wide open. Mist was drizzling into the room, along with chill twilight air.

Edging around the scatter of papers and envelopes on the

floor, Groucho gave the window frame a manly tug and shut out the cold. Narrowing his eyes, he looked down into the back acreage. There was no sign of anyone down there. Only a vast lawn and more trees and shrubs, all blurred by gray mist.

"Son of a gun," observed Laura as Groucho helped her settle into a fat leather armchair. "I'm supposed to do the suicide scene in *The Lonely Heart* over at Columbia day after tomorrow. How am I going to do that with a big hickey on my noggin? They borrowed, you know, Mike Curtiz to direct, and he's always chewing me out even when I don't have any blemishes."

"Makeup will cover it," Groucho said, sounding a shade avuncular. "Suppose you tell me what's been going on here, Laura."

"You tell me, buster. Can you hand me that cigarette box?"

He fetched the japanned box from the disordered top of the desk, handed it to her. "Who slugged you?"

"Search me." She selected a cigarette, and Groucho lit it for her.

"Would this have anything to do with the reason you called me?"

"You bet your fanny it does, Groucho." She exhaled smoke, coughed twice. "First I'll give you the lowdown on what went on here just now." She took another puff, coughed once more. "See, it's the servants' day off—it's kind of screwy, but I have five of 'em. Anyway, I got home from the studio about..." She checked her small platinum wristwatch. "Geeze Louise, it was only twenty-two minutes ago. I let myself in, and then I heard some funny noises from up here in the den."

"Such as?"

"Nothing real noisy, but like somebody was opening drawers and such," Laura told him. "So I came on up. Nobody's going to go snooping around my house."

"Breaking in on a burglar isn't too—"

"You're telling me." She rubbed at the bruise, gently, with the palm of her hand. "I yanked open the door, and I see a guy all dressed in black rummaging through my desk and tossing stuff every which way."

"Can you describe the fellow?"

"I know this sounds corny, Groucho, but I swear he was wearing a mask."

"That's wonderful," he said. "In all my years as one of Greater Los Angeles's best-loved amateur sleuths, I have never yet encountered a mysterious masked man. I was starting to feel neglected."

"Well, this bozo sure was. He had on black trousers, a navy blue turtleneck, and pulled over his head some kind of black hood," Laura continued. "Before I had a chance even to ask who the dickens he was, he lunges right at me and bops me on the sconce with a blackjack. As I'm sinking to the carpeting, this gink dives out the window. And that's one heck of a long drop down to the grounds."

"What do you think this mysterious intruder was after?"

"Obviously the little black strongbox."

"Which little black strongbox would that be, Laura my child?"

"Let's go down to the sunroom—even though it's sun-free today—and you can fix us a drink, and I'll explain the whole and entire screwy setup to you."

Laura sat in a mission-style armchair, a highball in her right hand and her left holding a petite ice pack to her bruised forehead.

Groucho, nursing a ginger ale, was on a gilded Victorian sofa.

The sunroom was large, with one entire wall made of sheets of faintly blue glass. About a dozen yards from the house was an Olympic-size swimming pool, tiled in turquoise and pale orange. A thin gray mist hung over the water.

"This all has to do with Randy, rest his rotten soul," she told Groucho. "I shed that crumbum three flapping years ago, and he's still giving me grief. From beyond the damn grave he's giving me trouble."

"I feel in need of a few more details."

"Sorry, but getting conked on the coco tends to make me dither," she apologized, taking a taste of her drink. "Okay, here's the scoop, kiddo. Randy was a louse, but a good-looking louse with plenty of sex appeal. So it took me over a year to get completely fed up with him. When we split, I vowed never to see him again. Ever."

"But you did?"

She sighed. "Yeah, it was because of a sob story he handed me," Laura explained. "Calls me up, out of the blue, and wants me to do a favor for him. He was in some kind of temporary trouble and needed my help. When I ask the lunk, 'Why me?,' he gives me a song and dance about how everybody knows I won't touch him with a barge pole and so they won't think of looking here for what he wants to stash for a spell."

"But today they did come looking."

"You hit the nail on the head," Laura said, readjusting her ice pack and wincing. "Ouch. I'm going to look lousy on camera, even with pancake. Where was I? Yeah, so this egomaniacal bastard drops over and hands me a black strongbox. Nothing big—about, oh, a foot or so wide and two or three inches deep. Locked up tight. He tells me there's some important documents inside and he's scared to have them around his dump just now."

"Did he tell you what was in the box—or why it was important?"

"Naw, but I can guess," she said. "Maybe you don't know this yet, Groucho, but in addition to being a crummy actor and a philanderer, Randy sometimes practiced a little blackmail on the side. My guess is that there's some incriminating stuff in the box and that maybe one of his clients was getting tough with him. I never tried to open the darn thing."

"He didn't tell you who or what he was afraid of?"

"He didn't, no," she said. "You know, Groucho, I didn't think I'd ever do that guy a favor, but there's something about him . . . make that *was* something about him . . . that once in a while could get to me. I made sure, by the bye, that the night he dropped over, all five of my servants were on call."

"And where's the box now?"

"Not in the den," she answered. "Did you know that Barney Kains, back when he was really in the chips, had seven—you heard me right, seven—different safes hidden in this joint. I stuck the box in one of those, and, so help me Hannah, I never once tried to pry the darn thing open. I want you to take it off my hands."

"Maybe the police would be a better—"

"Police, my fanny. I'm as deep in this whole frumus as I want to be," she said firmly. "You take it and open it. Maybe you'll find something inside that'll help you guys find out who killed the poor bastard. Maybe you'll even be able to establish that that bitch Dorothy Woodrow didn't do it."

"You're not fond of Dorothy?"

"Not so you'd notice, no. But that's another story." She held out her empty glass. "Fix me another drink before you take off."

Twelve

I watched Jane's face as she sampled her coffee. "Well?" I asked.

"You're improving," she decided. "But I wish I could convince you that I'm still in perfect condition to brew a pot of coffee. And probably wrestle the Swedish Angel and beat him two falls out of three."

"No doubt, but—"

A timid tapping sounded on the front door.

Rising up from his favorite patch of living room rug, Dorgan gave a tentative bark.

"This is the Easter Bunny," announced a fluty falsetto voice out on our porch. "Let me in quick before all these eggs go bad."

"Groucho," said Jane.

"Groucho," I said.

Our bloodhound trotted to the door, tail wagging.

I opened the door, and Groucho came bounding in, a black strongbox tucked up under his arm. "I'm with the Gallup Poll, folks, and we're interested in finding out how many people in your cozy little neighborhood wouldn't touch Groucho Marx with a ten-foot Gallup pole."

"Put us down for two," said Jane.

Nodding at the box, I asked, "What's in that?"

"I'm not, as will soon be revealed, certain." He placed the black box on the floor and settled into an armchair. "This could well be, Rollo—and Mrs. Rollo—a veritable Pandora's box. I'm referring to Isidore Pandora, who ran a notorious fish market in Queens and surrounded himself with boxes full of gefilte fish."

"Where'd you acquire it?" I sat next to my wife on the sofa.

"From the late Randolph Spellman's erstwhile wife, Laura Dayton, soon to be starring at a movie house near you in *The Son of Call of the Wild.*" To Jane he said, "You're looking well, Lady Jane. I wish to discuss the case with Franklin, but you can retire if you—"

"Despite what Frank says, I'm perfectly fit to listen to what you boys have to say about this whole business," she said, smiling. "I'm especially curious about the black box."

"Before I avail myself of Frank's exceptional abilities as a cracksman, I think we'd best compare notes and tote up what we've learned thus far."

I grabbed my notebook off the coffee table, flipped it open. "Here's what I got from May Sankowitz."

"Ah, yes, the petite Hollywood gossip who's brighter than Hedda Hopper and cuter than Louella Parsons," he said. "Although that isn't really saying much, is it?"

I filled him in on what my friend had told me. That she confirmed that Spellman had been blackmailing on the side, that Dorothy Woodrow had run up an impressive total of men friends in the past few years, and that the reason Arthur Wright Benson wanted to dump Spellman from the Ty-Gor movies was because he suspected the guy of having an affair with his latest, and much younger, wife. I tossed in the facts that Joe E. Brown had again been voted Most Lovable Movie Comedian and that Alicia Benson's beau had absconded with AWB, Inc., funds.

"I must say that I'm stunned that someone of my proven lovability didn't garner that Golden Orange." From an inside pocket of his sand-colored sports coat, Groucho withdrew a folded sheet of old hotel stationery.

He gave us a report of what he'd found out from Randy Spellman's agent, including the fact that Warlock had already picked a new actor to take over as Ty-Gor. Hershman was evasive about Spellman's sideline as a blackmailer, but didn't deny it. He knew about his client's affair with Mrs. Benson and was sure that's why old Benson wanted him fired, though the matter had never been mentioned directly. There was also a possibility that Randy had also made a play for Alicia Benson. The agent told Groucho he could think of a lot of people who wouldn't miss Spellman, but didn't care to speculate on who actually killed him.

"You think that's true about Randy and Benson's daughter?"

"My boy, keep in mind that Lew Hershman is an *agent*," he reminded. "Their credo calls for them to use the truth as rarely as possible. Still, I think it safe to say that Spellman was doing more than swinging from tree to tree out at Rancho Tygoro."

"Which," said Jane, "would give old Benson a stronger motive than Dorothy."

"It gives him a motive for trying to get Randy fired," I said, frowning. "But not necessarily for doing away with the guy."

Jane pointed at the strongbox with the toe of her shoe. "Now explain that thing, Groucho."

"First a short preamble, kiddies." He explained about the telephone call from Laura Dayton and told us what had happened during his visit to her mansion. "Not since I read *Nick Carter Solves the Mystery of the Poisoned Chicken Soup; or,*

Louis B. Mayer at Bay have I been so excited," he concluded. "I came this close to actually seeing a masked intruder." He held his thumb and forefinger about two inches apart. "By a strange coincidence, that also happens to be the length . . . Ah, but I shan't discuss that in mixed company. And I've been discovering lately that even when I'm all by myself, I'm in mixed company."

Patting Jane's hand, I stood up. "I'll fetch my lock picks." I headed into our bedroom.

"It must be a great joy to be married to a chap who can crack safes, Jane."

"I'm hoping he can transfer that ability to opening jars of baby food when the time comes."

I set the small tool case down. "I first acquired these while I was working on the *LA Times*."

"What did the police think?"

"It was a couple of Los Angeles cops who taught me how to pick locks," I said, bending to lift up the strongbox.

As I spread the contents out upon the coffee table, Groucho remarked, "Shucks, no doubloons."

The black box contained nothing but three business-size gray envelopes, none of them sealed.

"C'mon, let's see what's inside 'em," urged Jane.

Selecting an envelope, I shook out its contents. "As might've been expected."

Five snapshot-sized photos dropped to the table, along with five negatives. Each showed couples in what the tabloids would describe as compromising positions.

"Jack O'Banyon takes a flattering photo," observed Groucho,

tapping one of the photos. "And the young lady looks especially naked without her schoolbooks."

O'Banyon was a successful character actor who specialized in tough-guy parts. He was chummy with outfits like the German American Bund and ran an amateur cavalry group called the Silver Shirts. Groucho and I had had run-ins with him a couple times in the past.

"The terrible things people do," said Jane quietly.

Groucho said, "The basic instincts of a lout like O'Banyon aren't—"

"I don't mean sleeping with an underage girl, though that's bad enough," she said. "It's taking photographs of it that seems to me even worse."

"This looks like somebody from Vince Salermo's mob." I held another photo toward Groucho.

"Right you are, Rollo. That's a lad named Val Gallardo, and the lady peeking out from the covers is the current wife of a state senator named Levin."

None of us recognized any of the participants in two of the other pictures. The fifth photo showed an actress named Rochelle Shaye in bed with a man not her husband.

"We'll have to find out who these other sinners are." Groucho carefully gathered up the pictures and returned them to the envelope. "If this stuff bothers you, Jane, you—"

"Nope, since I prompted you to take on this case, I can stand to look at what you dig up. No matter how nasty."

"We can assume," I said, "that at least one of the folks in each of these pictures could have stood up to Spellman and gotten tough with him. O'Banyon sure might, and so would Gallardo."

"We can also assume that he was especially afraid of this

bunch and wanted what he had on them hidden elsewhere than his home."

Jane said, "Two envelopes to go."

The second envelope contained three folded newspaper clippings. They'd been cut from the *LA Times*.

The largest clipping, dated a few months earlier, had a headline reading, TY-GOR BOOKKEEPER SUSPECTED OF EMBEZZLING. That one also offered a headshot of a lean, youthful-looking fellow with short-cropped dark hair and a sincere necktie. The caption identified him as Doug Cahan. The two smaller cuttings were follow-ups: MISSING ACCOUNTANT SOUGHT. ABSCONDS WITH $15,000 and AUTHORITIES STILL SEEKING TY-GOR THIEF.

"How does this Cahan guy fit in with Spellman's extortion business?" I said after spreading the three newspaper stories out atop the table.

Groucho picked up the largest clipping and read it over. "The missing accountant, age twenty-eight, used to work for Ira Silverlake's accounting firm before joining the Benson outfit."

"And?" I inquired.

"Ira Silverlake is a lecherous old soul who somehow managed to become a member of the Hillcrest Country Club, which, as you well know, Rollo, proudly lists the name of Groucho Marx on its roster," he explained as he dropped the clipping. "It would be a nice idea to have a heart-to-heart chat with Ira, whom I'm certain I can locate at one of our fair city's finer bordellos if he's not in his office on Wilshire, and ask him about this Cahan lad."

"We ought to know more about this missing bookkeeper, yeah," I agreed.

"And more about why," added Jane, "Spellman thought he was important enough to stow in his black box."

"Could be," I said, "Spellman knew where Cahan had skipped to with the fifteen grand and was blackmailing him. Or, since the guy was Alicia Benson's sweetheart, maybe Spellman was blackmailing her."

"I shall take it upon myself," volunteered Groucho, "to track Ira Silverlake to his lair and gather more information on the elusive Cahan. And if there's time, I may gather a few rosebuds as well."

"So far no photos of Dorothy," said my wife. "That might mean Spellman wasn't especially afraid of her."

Inside the final gray envelope was a folded sheet of tablet paper.

Spread out atop the table, it looked to be a very crude map.

"Not much of a cartographer," observed Jane. "From the lettering, I'd say it was drawn by a man."

The drawing consisted of a few wiggly lines, dozens of tiny triangles, a lopsided oval, the N-E-W-S arrows in the lower corner, and a shaky dotted line running from near the oval to a big X between two trees. Lettered along the arrow was "21 feet 7 inches." A squiggly line across the top of the page was designated "back fence," and two parallel lines running down between the clusters of triangles had "road" written between them. Near the lower end of the clumsy map, a small rectangle among the triangles was labeled "hut."

Taking a closer look at the map, Groucho said, "What was our mapmaker, who I assume was Spellman, trying to depict?"

"Something he buried in the woods?" proposed Jane.

"You think the triangles are trees?" he asked.

"Some of them have tiny tails. That's the way lots of people draw Christmas trees."

"Meaning the late Ty-Gor hid something in a Christmas tree lot in the vicinity of an oval?"

"That oval might be a pond, which could mean the burial site is off in the woods someplace."

Setting down the map, Groucho leaned back in his chair. "Spellman thought this was important. Did somebody kill him because they wanted to get hold of it?" he said. "Or maybe because they didn't want anybody else to get hold of it."

"Be nice if we knew what was buried at *X*," I said.

"Or who," said Jane.

Thirteen

The morning was clear and sunny. Our kitchen was, therefore, bright and sun-filled. Jane, wearing a checkered smock, was sitting at the table with a stack of several-dozen fan letters in front of her.

I was over at the sink washing our breakfast dishes.

" 'Dear Sir, You are my favorite. Please send me an autograph,' " Jane read aloud.

"That's a very touching and personal message."

"It's also a carbon copy."

"Well, now that you've become a celebrity, autograph hounds have added you to their list." I thrust a plate into the drying rack.

Jane had opened another letter. "Ah, this is more like it," she said, waving the sheet of blue paper a few times. " 'Dear Jane, Your comic strip is very cute, and I'm betting you're a cutie, too. If you're ever in Youngstown, Ohio, I'd like to take you dancing.' "

"Proves they know how to pick women in Youngstown."

"Come here a minute," she requested.

Wiping my hands on a dish towel, I crossed the linoleum to her side. "More invitations?"

Jane pushed back in her chair, took my hand, and pressed it to her stomach. "She's kicking again."

"So she is." I could feel a faint fluttering. "Getting ready to escape, I'd say."

Jane put both her hands around mine. "Let me ask you a serious question."

"Is there a cash prize involved?"

"I'm serious, Frank."

"So am I, Jane. I don't intend to answer a bunch of questions, if there's no money to be—"

"Hush and listen up," Jane requested. "Do you find me at all attractive in my present bloated condition?"

"C'mon, Jane, you asked me this before, and you know darned well that—"

"I know, but I'm feeling very squatty and ugly just now."

"You're not. You're as pretty as—"

"Just pretty?"

"Okay, gorgeous, too."

"You're not just humoring me?"

"Jane, I love you, remember? To me you are always attractive, day or night, come rain or come shine."

"And you wouldn't rather be sleeping in the same bed with a slim, unpregnant woman about now?"

"Nope."

She sighed, releasing my hand. "Well, then I guess I'll quit brooding for a while."

Kissing her on the cheek, I said, "I must confess, though, that I've been dreaming about Carmen Miranda lately."

"That I can live with."

"Why don't you forget your fan mail for—"

The telephone rang.

I went into the living room, picked up the phone from the end table. "Hello."

"What progress are you guys making?"

"Some, Enery," I replied. "I'm going to be seeing another old *LA Times* coworker this afternoon to get some more information on something that's turned up."

"They haven't been saying much new in the papers," said Enery McBride. "It's been a couple days now."

"Your friend still staying put?"

"Sure, but this waiting to hear anything is—"

"You might reconsider our advice."

"No, that's not going to happen yet."

"I'll try to get back to you late this afternoon."

"Did you know they've hired a new actor to take over the Ty-Gor part?"

"I heard, yeah."

"Studio asked me to report tomorrow morning," said our actor friend. "We're going to shoot some of the cannibal village stuff."

"That's great. It means you're back on the payroll."

"Take more than that to cheer me up just now, Frank. Talk to you soon."

I hung up. "That was Enery."

The phone rang again.

"Yeah?"

"Is this Fred Dumphy?"

"Close. It's actually Frank Denby." I recognized the chill voice of my agent's secretary.

"I think Max Bickford walks to talk to you," she said, her

tone implying that why in the world a man of Max's stature in Hollywood would lower himself to talking to me mystified her. "Please, hold on."

After listening to silence for close to a minute, I heard Max asking, "Frank, how are you doing, buddy?"

"Splendidly, and yourself?"

"I think Onita borrowed my Mercedes again."

"You aren't certain?"

"It might simply be that I parked it someplace and forgot where. But, no, I'm darned near sure she's headed for the border with that hairdresser."

"Which hairdresser, Max?"

"You know, Maurice. He's the only hairdresser in LA who isn't a pansy."

Onita Sands, an actress whom Max had thus far only been able to place in a succession of Republic Pictures serials, was not exactly faithful enough to be called his steady girlfriend. She had an unfortunate tendency to borrow one of his cars and head off with one or another of her alternative beaus.

"I'll pass your problem on to Mr. Anthony. Now tell me why you called me, Max."

"Oh, yeah. Joel Farber over at Warlock wants to see you pronto, Frank," remembered my agent. "Get over there soon as you can, huh?"

"Can you tell me why?"

"They've resumed filming the Ty-Gor movie, with that lunkhead Carl Nesbit taking over the star part," Max said. "Joel thinks he's going to need a few script changes."

I sighed. "Okay. Bye."

Jane asked from the kitchen, "And what did Max want?"

"I've been summoned to Warlock. Not as an amateur detective but as a scriptwriter."

"Not another rewrite?"

"I fear so."

"And which old *Times* buddy are you calling on?"

"Larry Shell, the photographer," I answered. "Going to show him those two photos with the frisky folks we can't identify. He's taken pictures of just about everybody in Greater Los Angeles, and I'm hoping he can identify at least some of them."

"What have the police been finding out about the murder?"

"They haven't seen fit to confide in me."

"So call that Tandofsky guy and ask him, for Pete's sake."

"Later in the day, perhaps."

Off in the bedroom Dorgan barked, then came walking into the living room. Tail wagging, he went to the front door.

I opened the door. "Good morning, Myra."

My wife's assistant smiled and entered.

That morning Groucho, he later told me, was up with the lark. In his part of Beverly Hills, the lark never arose before 10 A.M.

As Groucho was striding manfully along the sun-drenched Sunset sidewalk toward his office building, a tourist couple stepped into his path.

The husband, a lean, weather-beaten man in his forties, was carrying a box camera.

His wife, equally lean, smiled shyly at Groucho. "Mr. Marx, we'd love to have a photograph of you in our living room."

"Okeydokey, the next time I'm in your living room, snap away."

"No, we want to take a picture now," explained the husband. "If that's all right with you, Mr. Marx?"

Groucho said, "Well, I suppose I can overcome my terrible shyness just this once." He sighed. "I was so shy in prep school that everybody called me a wallflower. And, speaking of flowers, it was even worse at college, where they called me a pansy. Where was I?"

"Is it okay to snap a picture of you?"

"Very well." Groucho slipped his arm around the woman's thin waist. "You'll add a little glamour to the shot, dear lady. Not to mention a generous dollop of schmaltz."

"That'll be swell." The husband clicked the camera.

Pressing his cheek to that of the somewhat-perplexed wife, Groucho suggested, "Take another one. You may want to use it on your Christmas cards this year."

Someone tapped Grouch on the shoulder. Without turning, he said, "One idolater at a time, if you don't mind. Soon as—"

"Pardon me, Mr. Marx, but Mr. Salermo kind of wants to see you right away. In a hurry, so to speak."

Hunching his shoulders, Groucho slowly turned. "My goodness, what a pleasant surprise."

Two tan young men in pinstripe blue suits and dark glasses were standing there. Groucho could detect the presence of a shoulder holster under the jacket of the huskier of the pair of hoodlums.

"Thank you very much, Mr. Marx," said the husband as he and his wife went hurrying away along Sunset Boulevard.

"Would you mind telling Vince Salermo that I've retired to Tangiers?" he asked the hoods. "Yes, tell him I've retired to Tangiers to raise tangerines and learn the tango."

"He doesn't intend to harm you in any way," the huskier one assured Groucho.

"Yet he'd be very miffed if you failed to accept his invitation to drop in," explained the smaller hoodlum.

"I can't begin to tell you how flattering it is to have one of the best-loved mobsters in Greater Los Angeles pay attention to little me," said Groucho. "But this is not an appropriate time. In fact, there's not a day in 1940 that looks good. How about trying again after the first of the year and—"

"Mr. Salermo made it clear to us," said the huskier one, "that we weren't to shoot you if you tried to turn him down."

"Or bop you with a sap."

"Or break any important bones. He did, however, give us permission to use some force to persuade you to pay this call on him right now, Mr. Marx."

"In that case, it would be churlish of me to refuse, and so I accept. Whereabouts is your boss?"

"We'll take you to him."

"Will I need my overnight bag and a toothbrush?"

"He's nearby, Mr. Marx."

"You're great at kidding around," observed the huskier one. "That's a swell way to be. But not always."

Fourteen

The long black limousine pulled to a stop next to a fire hydrant on Hollywood Boulevard. The smaller hood came back to open the rear door. "Walk this way, Mr. Marx."

"Ah, a perfect straight line, but I'm a little wary about following it up."

There was a brand-new shop just opposite. Inscribed on the window was AUNT FRANNY'S OLD-FASHIONED ICE CREAM SHOPPE. "In here," invited his escort, opening the door.

A friendly bell tinkled as Groucho entered. There were strawberry-pattern café curtains at the windows, over a dozen customers at the marble-topped tables, and the scents of chocolate, bananas, and chopped nuts thick in the air. Above the soda fountain that stretched across the rear of the parlor was a large blackboard on which was lettered, in colored chalks, FLAVOR OF THE DAY—ORANGE PAGO PAGO!

The young mobster guided Groucho to a rear door beside the fountain.

Pausing, Groucho leaned an elbow on the marble fountain top and inquired of the pretty blonde waitress, "Would you have anything in the way of chocolate matzos or an egg cream?"

"Through here," urged his escort, taking hold of his arm.

After traveling down a spotless white corridor, Groucho was ushered into a spotless white office.

Sitting at a Swedish-modern desk was Vince Salermo. He was a small, compact man in his middle fifties, deeply tanned and with wavy black hair that was possibly not his own. "You know what annoys the hell out of me about owning an ice-cream joint, Groucho?"

"Not always liking the flavor of the day?"

"Not being able to smoke." Salermo, who was the king of illegal gambling in all of southern California, stood up. "If I so much as take a few puffs of a cigar back here, they smell it out in the goddamn ice-cream parlor."

"Why are you in this business at all?"

"Branching out into another legit sideline," answered the mobster. "Sit down. Eventually I'll own a chain of these Aunt Franny dumps."

Groucho sat in a blonde chair.

In addition to Salermo, there were two other hoods in the room. Young men in dark suits, one on each side of the desk.

"Don't get the idea, Vincent," said Groucho, "that I don't enjoy these occasional visits. However, could we get our chat over with so I can continue on my rounds?"

"In a minute," promised Salermo, nodding at the hoodlum on his left. "What was that crap Nick came up with for tomorrow's special flavor?"

"Raspberry Vertigo," answered the young man.

"What do you think of that name, Groucho?"

"Makes me dizzy."

"You like ice cream?"

"Not especially. An egg cream, though, is something else

again. Well, obviously it's something else again, or it'd be an ice cream."

"Go get Groucho a sample of that raspberry crap from the test kitchen."

"Sure thing, boss." He left the office.

Groucho politely asked, "What was the purpose of kidnapping me, Vince?"

"All my boys did was invite you politely to drop over," corrected the gangster, chuckling. "Okay, now here's what I want to talk about, Groucho. I understand that you and your pal Frank are working on the Randy Spellman murder case. Am I right?"

"We already have a client, if that's—"

"Naw, I know how you guys operate. You don't take fees for being detectives," said Salermo, settling back into his pale desk chair. "All I need is a small favor."

"Such as?"

"While you're digging up dirt on Spellman, could you see if you can maybe find some stuff I'm interested in?"

"Not if it means a conflict of interest."

"All I want to find—"

"Excuse me, boss." The young hoodlum had returned carrying two dishes of a blue ice cream. "Nick got his dander up because you didn't like his Raspberry Vertigo, so he flushed it all down the sink. He's come up with a brand-new flavor for tomorrow—Banana Bonanza."

Salermo scowled at first one dish, then the other. "How come it's blue?"

"When I tried to ask Nick that, he threw an eggbeater at me."

Salermo asked Groucho. "You can't christen something that's blue Banana Bonanza, can you?"

"Not and keep the respect of gourmets. Now as to—"

"You two guys sample this stuff," he ordered his bodyguards, handing each a dish of the blue ice cream. "Groucho, I got a guy working for me by the name of Val Gallardo."

We had a photo of Gallardo in our collection. "I do believe I've heard tell of the lad," said Groucho. "Has a way with the ladies."

"That's him. Horny as a toad, but not especially smart and . . . what are you gargling for?" He frowned up at one of the bodyguards.

The young man pursed his lips, made a few throat-clearing noises. "This doesn't taste like bananas," he managed to say. He ran his tongue, which he noticed was now bright blue, over his lips and winced.

"Take this crap back to Nick and tell him to start over again." He made a shooing motion.

Both bodyguards, clutching their dishes of ice cream, left the office.

Salermo shook his head, muttered in Italian. "You'd think peddling ice cream would be fun," he said. "Anyway, Spellman had some pictures of Gallardo that he was using to blackmail the sap with."

"We've heard that Spellman had a profitable sideline. Paid even better, I'm reliably informed, than ice cream."

"Here's the favor, Groucho. If you guys come across any pictures of my boy in the sack with some dame he ought not to be in the sack with, I'd appreciate it if you'd keep the cops from seeing them," said the gangster. "And make sure that I got hold of them. Can you do that?"

Groucho held up his right hand. "You have my solemn oath, Vincent," he lied, "that any smutty snapshots of this amorous chap will find their way swiftly to you."

"I appreciate that, Groucho."

Groucho stood up. "Do you have any ideas about who killed Spellman?"

"We didn't do it," he assured him. "Gallardo didn't. But that leaves a lot of other people who hated the guy."

"How'd you find out your boy was being blackmailed?"

"He wasn't going to tell me. But a few weeks back he got a call from the blackmailers at one of my nightspots, and I answered it. After that, I saw to it that Gallardo confided in me."

"Blackmailers, plural?"

"The caller was a dame with a Scarlett O'Hara drawl, Southern belle stuff," answered the mobster. "From what Gallardo tells me, she'd made calls for Spellman before, but he's never laid eyes on her."

"Wellsir, it's been, once again, almost a pleasure chatting with you, Vince," Groucho informed him. "And I do hope you find a new flavor of the day before tomorrow rolls around. I know that nothing annoys me more than having to consume the same flavor of the day two days running. And even when I'm not running, it—"

"I'll see that some of my boys drop you off where they found you, Groucho," promised Salermo.

For a moment I thought another Ty-Gor had been murdered. A man in a leopard-skin loincloth was lying facedown at the edge of the Soundstage 3 indoor jungle. But as I drew nearer, I saw that he was moving, apparently doing push-ups.

Carl Nesbit was about the same build as Randy Spellman, and his hair had been dyed to match the shade of his predecessor. That way Warlock could use most of the Spellman long shots already filmed, and nobody, except a few astute movie buffs, would notice the difference.

When Nesbit ceased his warm-up exercising, a makeup man hurried over to him and started frowning at the actor's chest. Turning toward someone in the milling group of staff people, the makeup man asked, "Who in the hell shaved this guy's chest?"

No one admitted to it.

Nesbit, whose voice was a shade high-pitched for a jungle lord's, inquired, "Now what's wrong, Eddie?"

Eddie poked the new Ty-Gor's chest. "Stubble," he explained. "Here, here, *and* here."

"Who's going to notice a—"

"Arthur Wright Benson, God bless him. He insists on absolutely no body hair."

Nesbit shrugged, rubbing his fingertips over his recently shaved chest.

Spellman's trailer was gone, replaced by a slightly smaller one. That probably indicated that the studio didn't consider that Nesbit was quite as important as Randy had been.

Sitting on the steps leading up to the portable dressing room was Joel Farber. He was in the midst of an argument with a pretty, dark-haired young woman dressed in a scant costume composed chiefly of feathers and gauze.

"I am," she was saying in a fairly thick Spanish accent that I won't try to capture, "I am a goddess, Joel!"

"Only in the movie, Nova."

"In the movie, yes, I am a goddamn goddess," she said, angry, and pointing at the intricate feathered headdress she was wearing. "But you give me a headdress that is . . . how do you say it? . . . tacky. When I appear on the screen, all the critics— Hedda Hopper, Louella Parsons, Johnny Whistler—they'll say,

'There's Nova Sartain in a tacky headdress.' It's insulting to me."

"Hedda, Louella, and Johnny wouldn't be caught dead at a Ty-Gor screening, dear," my producer assured the enraged actress. "So you needn't worry about—"

"My fans, of whom there are multitudes, will gasp and exclaim, 'How dare Warlock dress our screen idol in such a tacky headdress?' They'll riot and tear up theater seats all across the country, Joel."

"I doubt that the majority of your fans give a damn, Nova."

"Is that an insult?"

"Nope, a mere statement of fact."

I kept at a distance, hoping that the debate would soon conclude and that I could find out what Joel wanted of me. While I was standing in the shadows, two stagehands grunted by, carrying one of the palm trees that Arthur Wright Benson had sent over on the day of Spellman's murder.

They hefted it over to the studio jungle and took it in among the other trees.

It occurred to me that the batch of trees had been delivered in some sort of large truck. It wouldn't have been too tough for someone to get smuggled onto the lot by hiding among the potted palms.

We'd have to look into that.

Whether this was a clever insight or what is commonly referred to as clutching at straws I wasn't sure.

Nova Sartain suddenly ripped off her feathered headdress, tossed it at Joel along with an impressive collection of insults in Spanish. Turning on her heel, she went striding off to her trailer. It was even larger than Spellman's, and there was a pale, frightened-looking girl in a maid's uniform standing uneasily in the doorway.

"You summoned me, Joel?" I asked, walking over to him.

"Frank, yes, I did." He stood up, and we shook hands. "Boy, I think that dame expects me to hire Edith Head to glue feathers on her ass. You understand Spanish?"

"Yeah."

"What'd she call me?"

"The usual. Why'd you send for me?"

"Some of the guys in the front office decided that we don't want very much funny stuff in this movie after all, Frank."

"And why is that?"

"I don't know. Respect for the dead, I guess," my producer explained. "They're going to stick a dedication at the beginning of the thing—saying something like 'To the memory of a great actor, Randolph Spellman.' It's bullshit, but that's what they want."

"What they don't want is Professor J. Darwin Underbrush and Groucho?"

He shook his head forlornly. "Afraid so, buddy," he said. "I need the new pages by next week. What you have to do, Frank, is cut out the comedy scenes, toss in a few sentimental touches. Replace the Groucho character with a serious explorer—or a white hunter. Guy might even be a missionary who's always mouthing off about how death is all around but we'll get our reward in heaven."

"How about a few angels dropping out of the trees and flapping their wings when Ty-Gor stumbles over a dead elephant?"

"Frank, you're a terrific writer. Put your mind to it, and you can give me a serious script. Okay?"

"Okay."

From Nova Sartain's dressing room came the sounds of things being thrown.

Joel took hold of my arm. "Oh, listen, there's one more thing, and don't blow your top over this, buddy."

"What already?"

"Arthur Wright Benson talked the front office into hiring an old pal of his for a couple weeks." He tried to look apologetic. "Old pulp magazine hack writer named Wallace Deems. Ever hear of the guy?"

"A few years ago," I replied. "Wait now, Joel. I'm not going to collaborate with him. Is that what—"

"Take it easy. Benson would just like Deems to do a little polish on your script. And on the new pages you're going to do for me."

"A polish? The guy who wrote stuff like 'Voodoo Queen of the Bayou' and 'The Loco Kid Rides South' is going to improve my script?"

"I don't like the idea much myself, Frank. But the front office wants to pacify Benson, so—"

"All right, okay."

"Fine, swell. I'd like you to go talk to Deems, long as you're on the lot," said Joel, giving me a tentative pat on the back. "He's over in the Writers Building. They stuck him in MacQuarrie's old cubbyhole."

After about a half a minute, I said, "I'll go over now."

"Terrific. Now everybody's happy."

"Almost everybody," I said.

Fifteen

His secretary scrutinized him as he came slouching in. "You're looking bedraggled."

"In point of fact, Nanette," said Groucho, removing his stogie from his mouth, "I'm bewitched, bothered, *and* bedraggled."

"Any particular reason?"

Perching on the edge of her desk, swinging one foot slowly back and forth, he replied, "I was dragooned. The chaps who did it weren't all that enthusiastic, later admitting that they were reluctant dragoons."

"They weren't outraged citizens who'd seen *At the Circus*?"

"No, they were torpedoes who invited me, rather politely, to visit good old Vince Salermo."

Nan sat up. "Are those gangsters bothering you again? When you and Frank were working on that Broadway murder case, Salermo—"

"I suppose I ought to be flattered. Salermo actually wanted to hire us."

"To commit what sort of crime?"

"To locate some incriminating photos of one of the more amorous members of his salon."

"And what did you say to Salermo?"

"Good-bye, as soon as I safely could," he answered. "He's in the process of opening an ice-cream parlor up on Hollywood Boulevard. That's where our rendezvous occurred."

Giving a sympathetic sigh, Nan picked up a memo slip. "Salermo isn't the only one interested in you and Frank."

"Let me see if I can guess. Is it Chiang Kai-shek? Elsa Maxwell? Wee Bonnie Baker? Two-Ton Tony—"

"Nope, it's Arthur Wright Benson."

Groucho's eyebrows went up. "The respected author of the Ty-Gor novels and owner of his own private jungle. My, my."

"Benson's son—who sounds like a true-blue twerp over the telephone—called to invite you and Frank to Rancho Tygoro for cocktails at 6 P.M. this evening, should you be available. The old boy wishes to discuss the progress of the Spellman case."

"I was under the impression that he felt nothing but disdain for Spellman. Of course, I was also under the table for a while there and may have missed something."

"According to sonny, the whole darn family is eager to see the killer brought to justice," Nan told him. "They didn't like Spellman as a person, but they consider the bumping off of the movie Ty-Gor an insult to the Arthur Wright Benson, Inc., empire."

"Here Frank and I have been searching high and low for suspects, and we could have just waited around for them to come to us."

"Oh, are any of the Bensons on your suspect list?"

"It would make things a lot simpler if they were," he said. "Six o'clock, you say?"

"Or thereabouts."

"I'll call Frank's place of residence to determine if he can join me on tonight's trek." Groucho reached for the telephone. "I, because of the monastic life I lead, am free this evening."

I was walking along the palm-lined street leading to the Writers Building when someone behind me called, "Wait up, Frank."

Turning on the late-morning street, I saw a pretty young woman whom I didn't recognize hurrying to catch up with me. She was wearing an open rayon bathrobe and a bright-flowered sarong. "Yes?" I said, trying to figure out who she might be.

The girl smiled. "I know, you don't recognize me." She held out her hand.

I shook it, admitting, "Afraid I don't, miss."

"I'm Polly Pilgrim," she told me. "I was the costar on the *Groucho Marx, Private Eye* radio show that you wrote."

"Polly Pilgrim? But . . ."

"Right, Frank. I used to be pudgy," she said. "And, back when you knew me, I had a different nose and different cheekbones, and my hair wasn't this reddish blonde. But that was over two years ago."

"Polly Pilgrim," I repeated, still surprised at the transformation she'd accomplished since she used to sing on our show. Groucho and I had cleared her actress mother of a murder charge, but since then I'd lost touch with both of them.

"I got myself a new agent about a year ago," Polly explained. "He sort of had me streamlined. His idea was basically that while I had a great voice, I wasn't exactly a knockout. I had to agree with him."

"So now you're a knockout," I said. "How's your mom taking all—"

"When I told her that Gene Thompson—that's my agent now, Gene Thompson—when I told her what he wanted to do, she said, 'This is Hollywood, honey. Do what you have to do, but try not to go to bed with anybody you don't like.' Sound advice."

I nodded. "That it is, Polly," I agreed. "You're working at Warlock now?"

"Gene got me a three-picture deal. Everybody thinks I'm going to be Warlock's answer to Deanna Durbin or maybe even Judy Garland."

"Or Gloria Jean."

"No, I'm going to do a heck of a lot better than she has," she said. "Being pretty has really built up my confidence. What are you doing these days, Frank?"

"Working on the script for the latest Ty-Gor movie."

"Seems like the movie's going to go on just fine without Randy Spellman," she observed. "How's your wife?"

"Expecting."

"When?"

"Any day now."

"Gee, that's swell." She shook my hand again. "Please say hello to Groucho. Oddly enough, I miss him." Leaning, she kissed me on the cheek and went hurrying away ahead of me.

"Polly Pilgrim," I said yet again, reflecting on the miracles that Hollywood can work.

Wallace Deems looked as though he'd been concentrating on doubling his weight over the past few years. He was in his early sixties, fat and pale, with a head of feathery silver hair. He overflowed his chair, and his size made his portable typewriter look somewhat like a toy. There was nothing else atop the desk except an ashtray holding a flock of cigarette stubs. "Enjoy it while you can, son," he said as I crossed the small, stuffy office.

"What, specifically?"

"Youth." He wheezed while shaking a fresh smoke out of his package of Camels. "How's your prostate?"

"Fine, far as I know."

Deems lit his newest cigarette, coughed, inhaled smoke. "Mine's the size of a watermelon," he said. "Or at least it feels that way. You get old, your prostate starts growing. It'll happen to you. Then either you can't take a pee, or all the livelong day you run to the can."

I sat in a rickety chair facing him. "Joel Farber tells me you're going to . . . do a polish on the script I'm writing for this latest Ty-Gor movie."

"Don't fret, son," the older writer advised me. "I fully intend to sit on my butt, collect my paychecks, and do as little work as possible. Art Benson, known to you as Arthur Wright Benson, is a pal of mine, and he finagled me this job."

"You still writing for the pulps?"

"Not so much these days, market's drying up. Back in the 1920s and early 1930s, I was banging out a million words a year," he informed me. "But my prostate gave out about the same time as most of my markets." He coughed again. "My specialty was exotic locales, which is why Art sold me to Warlock to work on Ty-Gor. If you own an encyclopedia and a good atlas, you can fake any damn exotic locale in the—"

"Then you don't intend to rewrite my stuff?"

"As little as possible."

Nodding, I asked, "How long have you known Benson?"

"A coon's age." Deems snuffed out his cigarette. "Met him back in New York about fifteen years ago. He was already cashing in with Ty-Gor, and I was grinding out my million words and living well out on Long Island. Art and I were drinking buddies."

"Now you're living in LA."

"Moved out a year or so ago, started scripting B movies," he said. "After you've plotted thousands of pulp yarns, putting together a cheapie action film is easy. I worked on a couple of serials for Republic, too."

"You and Benson are still close, huh?"

"I see him pretty often," said Deems, shaking his head. "Art's not all that happy these days. It's a big mistake, although I can see where it'd be tempting, to marry a pretty girl much younger than you are. They have a tendency to get restless."

"I've heard that, yeah."

He lit a fresh cigarette, then rested both his pale, flabby hands on the desktop. "This lad who got himself knocked off, this Spellman. He and Art's new wife were pretty chummy."

"Did Benson tell you that?"

"Not in so many words, but I could tell he knew what was going on," the erstwhile pulp writer said. "On top of everything, both of those kids of Art's are true pains in the butt. Especially Alicia."

"Oh, so?"

"Having a rich father can screw you up. I did a novelette about that for *Argosy* once, called 'Siren of the Snowdrifts,' where—"

"What about Alicia?"

"She's been man-crazy since she was out of rompers practically." He coughed out a swirl of smoke. "Ran away with one of the gardeners when she was still in high school. Some punk who was supposed to help tend that god damned jungle. Art had to hire some Pinkertons to drag her back from Tijuana, where she was shacked up with the guy. Worst of all, I think he was a Mex."

I stood up. "Anything you want to discuss about my script?"

"I read it, Frank, and it sounds great to me," he replied after coughing. "The new scenes will be fine, too. I'm just going to do a wee bit of tinkering, to justify my salary. Don't worry, son."

"I will strive not to."

"You also write that *Hollywood Molly* radio show, don't you?"

"Yeah, with some help from my wife."

"It's a pretty good show," Deems said. "But if I were you, Frank, I'd do something about the locales. Hollywood is okay, but think about using Hong Kong, Macao, Paris. Paris is especially easy to fake."

"I'll keep that in mind," I said.

Sixteen

I was still working for the *Los Angeles Times* when its new headquarters were built on West First Street. It's a massive building, granite below and cream-colored limestone on the higher floors. There's a bronze eagle on the roof.

As I walked by the place that morning, I didn't feel any nostalgia for the bygone days when I was a crime reporter on the paper. What I felt was happy that I'd moved on, that writing radio scripts and jungle man movies was closer to what I wanted to do.

My pace automatically kicked up, and I had the fleeting feeling that some circulation sluggers might come charging out of the *Times* building to press me back into service as a reporter.

My destination was a small café just around the corner.

Larry Shell, thin as ever, was waiting for me at a back booth in the Five Star Coffee Shop. "Is this going to result in a scoop for me?" asked the photographer.

I sat opposite him. "Someday, certainly. Right now, though, it gives you a chance to do a noble service for the cause of justice and—"

"Okay, since you're a longtime friend, I'll help you out of

115

the kindness of my heart," Larry said. "Has this to do with the Spellman murder that you and Groucho Marx are messing around with, huh?"

"That's right, yeah."

"Who do you think killed him?"

"It definitely wasn't Dorothy Woodrow."

"Nope, she's too sensible for that," he said, "and she never sticks with one guy long. Matter of fact, I took her out a few times couple years ago. Long before she got tangled up with Ty-Gor."

I took an envelope out of the breast pocket of my jacket. "What I'd like you to do, Larry, is take a look at a couple of photos and tell me if you can identify any of the people."

"What'll you have, kiddo?" A waitress of about sixty, with flamboyant red hair, had materialized in the aisle.

"Just coffee."

"You sure you don't want what your pal's having?"

I glanced down at Larry's plate. "I don't think so, no, but I'm not exactly sure what it is."

"That's the Five Star Special," she explained. "Consists of a glazed donut, topped with a scoop of vanilla ice cream, sprinkled with walnuts, and saturated with maple syrup."

"Reluctantly, I'll pass. Coffee."

"You'll regret it." She patted me on the shoulder and retreated.

Sliding the envelope across the tabletop, I said, "These are . . . well, photographs used for blackmail."

"Ah, dirty pictures." He picked up the envelope. "Doubt that they'll shock me."

"These came from Spellman's collection. They show people he considered, we think, important targets and dangerous ones. It could be that someone in the pictures had something to do with killing Randy."

Larry extracted the two small photos from the envelope, placing them side by side on the table. He rested his right hand next to them to act as a shield. "Well, that's interesting."

"Which one?"

"The pudgy guy in this shot is a very well-to-do real estate developer named Galen Klein. The lady I don't know, but she isn't his wife."

"I've heard of Klein. What about the other shot?"

"The woman lacking clothes is Mrs. Alden Poirier, and I'm pretty sure that fellow so intimately entangled with her was her chauffeur until about a month ago, when he got arrested for burglary." Larry returned the pictures to their envelope. "I've taken her picture several times in the past few years, mostly at fashionable charity dances. Her hubby is *the* Alden Poirier."

"Owns a baseball team."

"That's the guy. And his daddy has a nice collection of oil wells in Oklahoma."

"Makes Mrs. Poirier a nice subject for blackmail."

"So blackmail was Randy Spellman's sideline. I've heard rumors to that effect."

"Could be acting was his sideline, with blackmail his main source of revenue," I said, putting the envelope away.

The Golden State Hotel was not that far from the *Times* building in the tacky heart of Los Angeles. To the left of its once-resplendent façade was a boarded-up saloon named Big Bob's Nitespot, which sported a faded sign proclaiming, UNDER NEW MANAGEMENT! On the other side was a small dusty shop offering ALMOST NEW! clothing.

A very thin man who looked much older than he could

possibly have been was leaning in the shop doorway. "I got the perfect necktie for you, mister," he called out as I headed for the hotel's tarnished revolving door.

"Sorry, my wife just bought me the perfect necktie."

"Wouldn't hurt to try it on."

"Nevertheless." I went into the Golden State.

The lobby was vast and lofty, chock-full of heavy nineteenth-century couches and armchairs. For some reason the whole place smelled not of dust and decay but of fresh flowers. Well, more like funeral parlor flowers.

A man who looked even older than the neighboring haberdasher was sitting in one of the armchairs. He had a dented tea tray across his lap and was dealing out Tarot cards while muttering surprised noises. "Watch out for a woman you think you can trust," he told me as I crossed to the desk.

"I do that automatically, thanks."

The clerk was a boy of about twenty, reading a copy of a movie magazine. "I'd like to meet this May Sankowitz," he confided, sitting up. "She really knows Hollywood, and I bet she could show you a good time."

"At the very least. What room is Tim O'Hearn in?"

"You ever meet her?"

"No, but I once caught a glimpse of her on Hollywood Boulevard. It fair took my breath away. O'Hearn's room?"

"Three-thirteen," answered the young clerk. "Some people think that's an unlucky number, but O'Hearn says he's already had his lifetime quota of bad luck, and it doesn't matter." He returned to reading May's gossip column.

The ancient elevator, which smelled of both flowers and ancient urine, carried me, with several rattling lurches, up to the third floor.

The door of 313 was open about three inches. I stood near the slice of dim light. "O'Hearn. It's Frank."

"C'mon in," he invited. "Don't shut the door. I keep it open for ventilation."

His latest hotel room was much like all the other hotel rooms my old *LA Times* tipster had resided in over the years that he'd been supplying me with information. Small, musty, all the shades pulled down.

"You've changed your menu again," I noted.

"I was reading an article in *Time* at the all-girl barbershop across the street, Frank," explained O'Hearn, who was sitting on the edge of his unmade bed. "A respected doctor advised that a vegetarian diet was beneficial."

I lifted a paper plate that held the moldering remains of a nutburger off a faded armchair and sat. "Where do you find vegetarian fare?"

"There's a dinky Armenian joint up near Pershing Square." His foot nearly squashed the moss-covered unfinished nutburger that sat on the thin carpet as he started to leave the bed. "Want a beer?"

"Nope. What have you found out about Val Gallardo?"

"Think I'll have one." Both he and the bed creaked as he left it.

O'Hearn usually kept his beers in the tank of the toilet. He went into the bathroom now to fetch one.

"Okay, so?"

Picking a rusty bottle opener off his pillow, he opened the brown bottle of Regal Pale Beer. "Salermo's boy Val Gallardo didn't bump off Spellman."

"Then we can cross him off our list of potential killers. For now."

O'Hearn took a swig of his beer. "The word is—and I checked this in my usual thorough way, Frank—that Gallardo had nothing to do with bumping off that second-rate actor," he informed me. "Oh, by the way, you owe me ten bucks."

"Instead of the five we agreed on over the telephone?"

After coughing into his fist, O'Hearn drank some more of his Regal Pale. "I found out some other stuff," he said. "If you're interested."

Taking out my wallet, the one Jane's aunt in Fresno had sent me on my birthday, I gave my informant a ten.

He folded it twice, tucked it into his shirt pocket. "I found out that this guy Spellman wasn't working his blackmail dodge alone."

"And?"

"There was a mystery woman in the picture."

"Since she was a mystery woman, I suppose you couldn't find out her name?"

"No, but the word is Spellman had a dame who did some of his threatening for him." He paused to finish his beer. "Maybe two dames, because one of them had a Deep South accent."

"Or one dame with a gift for mimicry."

He went into the bathroom for another beer. "Sure you won't have one, Frank?"

"Absolutely convinced. Did you learn anything else?"

"Hell, pal, you already got fifteen bucks worth of inside dope for ten bucks." He returned with a bottle of Lucky Lager Beer. "Want me to keep nosing around?"

"Not on Gallardo. That looks like a dead end." I left the chair, nearly tromping on yet another mossy nutburger. "But if you hear anything else about this mystery woman, let me know."

"How much?"

"Another five."

"Jesus, Frank, haven't you heard the damned Depression's over? Wages are going up."

"Okay, ten if it's something we can use."

He uncapped the bottle. "I think this vegetarian diet is really working," he said. "I'm feeling a lot better. How do I look?"

"You're pretty close to looking alive."

"See, that's an improvement," O'Hearn said.

Seventeen

As we drove farther into San Fernando Valley, we left much of civilization behind—or what passes for civilization in and around Los Angeles—and found ourselves traveling past fields and ranches and occasional small towns.

First off, I explained to Groucho that Warlock was dropping his walk-on part in the Ty-Gor movie. "They think humor isn't appropriate to a movie they're now planning to dedicate to the memory of Randy Spellman."

"Alas, what's left for me now but a declining career as a dress extra?" he remarked, with a pathetic sigh. "Well, I'll certainly have more time to work on that crazy quilt I've been putting together. The only trouble is, two noted Rodeo Drive psychiatrists have warned me that my quilt is dangerously crazy and should be sent somewhere for observation. I was thinking of letting it be observed in one of the windows of the May Company department store. Or I may ship it to Topeka."

"Sure, the Menningers will straighten it out," I said. Next I filled Groucho in on what Larry Shell, Wallace Deems, and Tim

O'Hearn had told me and went over the now-expanded list of Randy Spellman's blackmail targets.

He inquired, "Would it be useful to find out if any of the folks on the list happened to visit the Warlock studios on the day of the murder? If so, I can take care of that tomorrow."

"It couldn't hurt."

"Have you ever seen blue ice cream?"

"Is that the title of a new novelty tune—like 'Have You Ever Seen a Dream Walking?' "

"No, it's a preamble to my account of my earlier audience with Vince Salermo."

"Jesus, him again."

Groucho recounted what had taken place at the Aunt Franny ice-cream emporium and of Salermo's interest in finding the blackmail stuff pertaining to his henchman Val Gallardo. "Who, according to your reliable sources, did not have anything to do with sending Spellman on to glory."

It was hot in the late-afternoon Valley, and I was perspiring. "I'm not often given to premonitions," I began, wiping my forehead with my pocket handkerchief. "But I—"

"I'm often given to palpitations myself, but that's not exactly the same thing." Groucho was hunched slightly at the wheel of his Cadillac. "And once I gave a dime to a little old lady selling violets in front of the Brown Derby. It turned out Violet was her daughter and the whole affair was rather . . . Are you having a premonition now, Rollo?"

"I keep feeling that Enery's not going to end up happy."

"Because his lady friend will turn out to be guilty of dispatching Spellman?"

I shook my head. "No, not that, Groucho," I said. "But I'm finding out that she's had affairs with quite a few guys and—"

"But only one at a time," he reminded. "That doesn't make her promiscuous, only a mite fickle."

"That can still end up hurting Enery or—"

"Here's where we turn for Rancho Tygoro." He guided the car onto a side road.

"By the time this case is cleared up, she'll probably move on to somebody else."

"This is Hollywood, where all life is conducted like musical chairs."

"I know, yeah, but—"

"We are the firm of Marx and Denby," he observed. "Not Miss Lonelyhearts and Beatrix Fairfax. We, most times, solve mysteries. We do not mend broken hearts. I'll now officially change topics. Is Jane feeling well?"

"She's fine," I said. "Tonight her assistant is going to be working late, so she'll be with Jane until I get home. I feel better if there's somebody with her at night."

Up ahead in the afternoon loomed a high stone wall with a wide, heavy wrought-iron gate. Groucho tapped the brakes, slowing the car. The words RANCHO TYGORO were writ large in copper letters over the gates. Stopping, he honked the horn.

A bearded man wearing a hunting jacket and riding breeches swung the gate open, then came striding toward the Cadillac. He was carrying a rifle under his right arm.

"Thank the Lord the hunting season for Marxes doesn't open until next month."

The man frowned in at Groucho. "Who're you?"

"I hate to admit it in public like this, but I'm Groucho Marx. My faithful companion is Frank Denby. We've been invited for cocktails, and later we're planning to swing from the trees for about a half hour or so."

The guard said, "You're in for a fun-filled evening, even without the trees." He turned, walked away, and opened the gates wider. Using the barrel of his gun as a pointer, he invited us to enter and drive on.

We did.

Eighteen

The house and buildings were a quarter mile from the entrance to the estate. The wide, graveled drive wound through vast green lawns and rows of diligently maintained shrubs.

The main house was in the mission style and at least twice as big as any real California mission. It was rich in slanting red-tile roofs and thick adobe walls. A few hundred feet to the right of the main house was a smaller building constructed along similar lines and with ARTHUR WRIGHT BENSON, INC., in bold crimson-and-gold lettering on its wide redwood door.

Groucho parked the car near the five-car garage, which was also in the mission style. "That's some home garden," observed Groucho as he left the Cadillac.

Rising up behind the buildings and stretching for acres into the distance was an immense jungle. There were high palm trees, as well as an assortment of other tropical trees that I didn't know the names of but had seen in many a jungle epic over the years. Vines and exotic blooms were thick and flickering above the green leaves, and in among the jungle shadows were bright tropical birds. And I was pretty certain I'd seen a monkey jump from sunlight into shade.

Midway between the publishing offices and the main house was a tall flagpole, from which fluttered the American flag, the California bear flag, and a pennant that simply displayed the letters AWB. Just to the left of the pole stood a life-size bronze statue of Ty-Gor. The jungle man held a knife high in his right hand, and his bare left foot was resting on the back of a slain leopard. A plaque at the base read, THE IMMORTAL TY-GOR, CREATED BY ARTHUR WRIGHT BENSON.

Pausing to gaze at the statue, Groucho said, "I wonder how I'd look in bronze. No, I'd probably get restless posing, and so, no doubt, would the leopard."

Before I could reply, the front door of the house came flapping open. "You can go straight to hell, Jack," said the angry blonde young woman who came rushing out into the late afternoon. "You're a no-good shit."

She paid us no heed, brushing against Groucho and running toward the garages.

"Alicia, you're being damned foolish about . . . oh, hello, Groucho." Jack Benson emerged from the big ranch house. "And Frank. My father will be pleased to know you're here."

"And your sister?"

"Oh, Alicia is just having one of her tantrums. It has nothing to do with you fellows."

A garage door automatically growled open, and a small yellow roadster came roaring out and headed for the gates of the estate.

My father will join us any minute now," Jack Benson told us, scratching absently at his nose. His sunburn was beginning to peel there.

He'd escorted Groucho and me into a large, lofty living room. The walls were an off-white stucco, and thick, darkwood beams crisscrossed the high ceiling. The chairs were of raw wood and leather. Hanging over the deep stone fireplace was an oil painting of Marge Benson, AWB's current wife, that was done in a manner somewhere between John Singer Sargent and a pulp magazine cover artist. She was a pretty woman with chestnut hair and a somewhat petulant look. The bookcases contained a wide range of novels, including what looked to be a complete collection of Benson's Ty-Gor books in every language they'd ever been printed in.

"Let me fix you fellows a drink," Jack offered with just a trace of cordiality.

Groucho settled into one of the wood-and-leather chairs. "Ginger ale."

"How about you, Frank—something a little stronger?"

"Plain seltzer."

Looking disappointed, Jack crossed to the liquor cabinet. "I hope it won't offend you teetotalers if I mix myself a Manhattan."

"Anything you desire," said Groucho as he drew a cigar from his coat pocket.

"You know," said AWB's son while opening a bottle of Canada Dry ginger ale, "it wasn't my idea to invite you to the ranch, Groucho."

"Being a part-time detective, I'd already deduced that."

Jack poured ginger ale into two sturdy crystal goblets. "We're all out of seltzer, Frank, so I'm afraid you'll have to settle for ginger ale. Or is that too strong for you?"

"I can handle it," I replied. "Why exactly did your sister make such an intense exit?"

"None of your damned business really." He tossed a few ice

129

cubes into each glass of ginger ale and left them sitting on the sideboard while he mixed himself a Manhattan. "Where the hell did they hide the cherries?"

Getting up, Groucho crossed over to him. He picked up our two glasses, delivering one to me. "I think I ought to warn you, young sir," he said in Jack's direction, "that while I am a dedicated disciple of Mahatma Gandhi and believe in nonviolence, Frank here is a direct descendant of the Clan MacDenby. He can accept no more than . . . how many is it, Franklin?"

"Three."

"The lad can accept no more than three personal insults before he's obliged to fetch his claymore . . . whatever that might be . . . and start cracking skulls. He's also available for cracking walnuts during the holiday season."

"He'd better not lay a hand on me," warned Jack, "or I'll have him thrown off the estate and barred from Warlock."

"Easy now, Son." Arthur Wright Benson had entered the room. He was a tall, balding man in his middle sixties, tan and wearing a tweed suit with leather patches on the elbows. "You won't do anything like that, and you well know it. Good evening, Groucho." He held out his hand.

Groucho shook it. "Now that we've gotten the majority of the insults and threats out of the way," he told the author, "perhaps we can get to your reason for inviting us to your rancho."

"Let me apologize for my son's—"

"I'm thinking of getting a spread like this for myself, though with no jungle attached," Groucho continued. "I plan to christen it Rancho Groucho, which has a nice ring to it. Of course, my nicest ring was the one I got from Jack Armstrong for a dime and a Wheaties box top. Darn thing glowed in the dark, told you where the North Pole was, and played 'The Light Cavalry Overture.'"

Benson suggested, "Let's go into my den, gentlemen. Jack, get over to the offices and take care of that dust jacket problem, will you? Tell them I want a lot more yellow, and we need it by Monday at the latest."

"I thought I was going to sit in on this confab with these road-show gumshoes."

"You're not, no," his father told him.

Arthur Wright Benson's den was overrun with dead animals. The paneled walls were decorated with the mounted heads of two elk, a moose, a bear, and a lioness. In a shadowy corner behind Benson's big oaken desk stood a stuffed gorilla, arms raised above its head and glass eyes glaring red. On the hardwood floor there were at least six animal-skin rugs, including a zebra, a tiger, and a spotted leopard. Two walls were given over to bookshelves holding more copies of AWB's novels along with bound volumes of the Ty-Gor comic book. Movie posters for the Ty-Gor motion pictures, dating as far back as 1928, hung in pale wooden frames on one wall. The other wall was crowded with framed inscribed photos of a variety of celebrities ranging from Herbert Hoover to Jean Harlow.

"My wife," explained the author, somewhat apologetically, as he took his place behind the neatly ordered desk, "is a bit under the weather tonight and sends her regrets. She's been a real fan of the Marx Brothers pictures since she was in high school." He gestured at the floor. "She fancies herself an animal lover, which is why I keep all my animal trophies in here and not in the living room."

"Did you shoot all these critters yourself?" inquired Groucho from the leather armchair he'd chosen.

Benson shook his head. "Regrettably I no longer have much time for hunting," he confessed. "I bought most of these from a taxidermist in Pasadena."

I asked, "Why exactly did you want to see us?"

He said, "Let me first apologize for my son's behavior. He and my daughter both have tempers, and at times it gets the better of them."

"I'm wondering," said Groucho, "why you're interested in Spellman's murder. I was under the impression you were trying to dump the fellow."

Resting both palms on his desktop, Benson said, "I was of the opinion that Randy was no longer in any shape to play Ty-Gor. But to millions of loyal fans he *was* Ty-Gor. As the creator of the most popular jungle hero in the world, I obviously think of Ty-Gor as one of the family. Therefore, I feel obliged to make certain that the killer of the man who represented my character to so many be brought, swiftly, to justice."

"We're already," I pointed out, "looking into Spellman's murder."

"I'm aware of that, Frank. What I'd like to see happen is you and Groucho keeping me informed on your progress. If you will, I'd also like to help finance your investigation."

"As odd as it may seem," Groucho told him, "we don't charge any fees. With us this is merely a sideline. Before that it was a chorus line, but our legs gave out."

"As for filling you in on our progress," I added, "we're not at the stage where we can discuss what we might suspect. And we're a ways from proving anything."

Benson glanced over his shoulder at the angry stuffed go-rilla. "I see," he said slowly. "Well, there is one other favor I'd like to ask."

"I'm not available to take over the role of Ty-Gor," Groucho said. "If that's the favor."

"My wife, Marge, is a sometimes-volatile woman," he said. "She's still quite young and a very outgoing creature." He rose to his feet. "You may hear rumors about her. Stories that she and Spellman were more than just friends. Have you?"

"No," Groucho lied.

"No," I lied.

"You may eventually," said Benson. "I can assure you the sto-ries are completely untrue, and I'd appreciate it if you didn't pay them any attention."

"In one ear and out the other," promised Groucho. "Or, in my case, in one ear, out a nostril, back in the other ear, and out a different orifice entirely. That is known in both medical and ge-ographic circles as the Scenic Route."

Benson came around to the front of his desk, resting one foot on the head of the leopard rug. "I've enjoyed talking to you gen-tlemen," he assured us. "Since you won't accept a fee, let me give you each an autographed copy of *Ty-Gor and The Sunken City.* That's number twenty-one in the ongoing series of Ty-Gor novels."

"I'm almost overwhelmed by the gift." Groucho stretched up out of his chair. "I'm sure my colleague is as well."

"I believe I'm actually even closer to overwhelmed than you, Groucho."

Taking two yellow-covered copies of the novel off a nearby shelf, the author distributed them to us. He opened the door of the den. "I'm afraid it's a little late to give you the grand tour of my jungle," he said. "But you both must come back someday soon and do that."

"I for one shall," Groucho promised. "Several people have told me to go climb a tree of late, and this will be my chance."

Nineteen

I was up at the true crack of dawn the next morning. While Jane slept, Dorgan and I, after I fed him and took him for a short walk in the gradually warming morning, settled down in my office.

Page 7 of the 27-page *Hollywood Molly* radio script, due the following Tuesday, was still awaiting me in my typewriter. Hunching slightly, tapping my lower front teeth with the eraser end of my favorite mechanical pencil, I read aloud what so far existed on the page.

JERRY WARBLER (on filter mike): My next exclusive item concerns cinema cowpoke Sam Wyoming, currently starring in the Republic oater *Deputy Sheriff of Devil's Door-knob*. Sam, minus his Stetson, was spotted last night at a movie-land hot spot wining and wooing moompitcher up-and-comer Marsha Invader. . . . Does that mean he's tossed his longtime tootsie, Molly McKay, soon to be seen in the musical remake of *Lost Horizon,* entitled *Tiptoe Through Tibet,* aside? Now an open letter to—
SOUND: Click of radio being turned off.

MOLLY: Sam, I know the studio made you take out that starlet, but you might have told me about it.

SAM: Well, shucks, Molly.

MOLLY: Instead I have to find out from that dippy movie gossip Jerry Warbler.

SAM: Well, shucks, Molly.

"So what do you think, Dorgan? Is that up to my usual hilarious standard?"

"Sounds fine to me, but I could be prejudiced." Jane, wearing the bathrobe her aunt in Fresno had made for her, was standing in the doorway.

"You feeling okay?"

"Fine, but I was having trouble sleeping with our forthcoming daughter tap-dancing within." She came into the room. "Good morning, Dorgan."

Our bloodhound wagged his tail, made pleased woofing noises as my wife settled into the room's sole armchair.

"I'll make you some coffee," I offered, pushing back from my desk.

"No, no," Jane said, making a stop-right-there gesture with her right hand. "I've already started a pot of coffee. It's not that your coffee is especially noxious or—"

"I thought you told me my coffee-making was improving."

"But improving at an awfully slow rate."

"Okay, I'm a big-enough hombre, as Sam Wyoming would say, to take a little honest criticism, ma'am."

Jane smiled. "I was thinking about what you told me about your visit to Rancho Tygoro last night."

"Have you come up with any ideas?"

She shrugged one shoulder. "More a far-fetched notion," she said. "Anyway, has it occurred to you that Benson's jungle has rows and rows of trees in it?"

"Sure, I noticed that last . . . wait a minute," I said. "You mean the Tygoro jungle could be the woodland on Spellman's homemade map?"

She nodded. "Is there a pool or a small lake in that jungle?"

"We didn't get a chance to tour the jungle, but old Benson invited us to come back sometime," I answered. "Yeah, and Spellman was out there quite a bit when they were filming *Ty-Gor and the Leopard Queen.*"

"So it's possible the guy could've buried some of his steamier blackmail stuff there, twenty-one and a half feet from the pond . . . if there is a pond," Jane suggested. "Or he maybe saw somebody else hiding something in the jungle."

"We're going to have to take a look around, just in case."

Jane got up slowly. "Think I'll fix myself some oatmeal."

"I can do that."

"Hey, you stay here and work on the darn script. I'll take care of breakfast."

As she was crossing the living room, the telephone rang.

Jane answered. "Hello. Yes, Enery. No, we're both awake," she said. "What's that? Okay, I'll tell him. I'm sure he'll get over there as soon as he can. Take it easy, and try not to worry." Hanging up, she came back into my office.

"What's wrong?" I asked her.

"That was Enery, and it sounds like Dorothy has disappeared again," she told me.

Being near the telephone reminded me that I ought to call May Sankowitz, since she hadn't yet sent me the promised list of other possible Randy Spellman blackmail targets. I gave the operator the number of May's *Hollywood Screen* magazine office.

"May Sankowitz," she answered,

"Frank Denby. Where's the—"

"Have you and Groucho caught the killer?"

"Not as yet, but what I—"

"Are you about to rush Jane to the maternity ward?"

"Wrong again, May. Now here's a question for *you*," I said into the phone. "Where the hell's that list you were supposed to send me?"

"Shit, I forgot, Frank," she said. "Hold on, I've got it on my desk someplace. Here's a fawning note from Cecil B. DeMille, some glossy shots of Nova Sartain almost wearing a bathing suit, a carrot, and . . . ah, here's the list."

May read five names to me. Three of them we already had, though I didn't mention that to her. "Thanks, May. But isn't the fifth victim dead? Sir Nigel Reesner, noted British import, expired last summer."

"So he is, died after he finished costarring in *The Return of the Bengal Lancers*. Excuse it," she said. "Don't you have even one item of news for me, dear?"

"Well, I keep hearing rumors that I'll be awarded the Nobel Prize for Hack Writing this year. But don't quote me."

"You're a wiseass, but I love you still. Good-bye."

Cradling the receiver, I took out my notebook and added the name of Arturo Paiva, the middleweight boxer, to our list of possible Spellman blackmail victims.

Looking at what I was jotting down, Jane said, "Paiva can't be a suspect. He's been in New York for nearly two weeks training for a fight coming up at Madison Square Garden."

I drew a line through the prizefighter's name. "Okay, I'm off to call on Enery."

"Tell him to cheer up."

"Why should he cheer up?"

"You're right," she said. "There's no earthly reason, is there?"

There were more than twenty pickets gathered in front of the Warlock studios entrance as Groucho drove up. Five of them were in the uniform of the pro-German Silver Shirts, although Groucho didn't spot Jack O'Banyon, the actor who'd organized the group, amongst them. The rest, mostly men, were in civilian garb. The large signs they were wielding had been professionally lettered.

Among the sentiments expressed were IT'S UN-AMERICAN TO BE ANTI-GERMAN!, STOP FILMING "HITLER'S SPY"!, WARLOCK IS A JEWLOVER!, and HITLER IS OUR FRIEND!

"Looks like the loony bin class picnic," Groucho said as he stopped at the entry.

One of the picketers, a husky blonde fellow in a Silver Shirt uniform, noticed Groucho. Pointing to the Cadillac, he yelled, "There's Groucho Marx! Another lousy anti-Nazi!"

Groucho was about to roll his window down to make a reasoned reply when an abundantly ripe tomato came squashing against the glass.

"If this was Germany, they'd put you away!" a fat matron cried, preparing to use her picket sign as an axe on his windshield.

One of the studio guards came running toward the car, his hand pressed against his holster. "None of that. All of you move back and let Mr. Marx pass, or I'll get the cops after you!"

Groucho drove on into the studio grounds.

He sat in the visitors' parking lot for several minutes, breathing slowly in and out through his open mouth. "If this were Germany, I'd be in a boxcar about now."

He sighed, took a cigar out of his coat pocket. Sighing again, he dropped the cigar back and stepped out of his car. He could still hear the protestors shouting out on the sidewalk.

He looked ruefully at the remnants of tomato that were slowly oozing down the driver's-side window. "Look on the bright side," he advised himself. "It could've been a brickbat."

He started for the Warlock Administration Building.

Groucho had covered about a hundred yards when he encountered a group of people coming his way. Four men and a woman were following a suntanned young man in a checkered sports coat.

"Wow, folks, here's a surprise treat for you!" he said, grinning.

Groucho halted. "I give up, what is it?"

"Folks," announced the amiable young man in the checkered coat, "this is Groucho Marx himself."

"I used to be Groucho Marx herself, but all the fellows at the club kept razzing me about it," he said.

"I'm Mark Glidden," said the young man, holding out his hand. "I'm escorting these newspaper movie reporters on a tour of the studio. Right now we're on our way to Soundstage 5 to watch them filming a scene from *Hitler's Spy*, starring Francis Lederer, Ida Lupino, and newcomer Laird Cregar. It's a suspenseful thriller that deals in an up-to-the-minute way with the activities of the Nazi spies in our very midst."

"Don't let me detain you," said Groucho, not bothering to shake Glidden's hand.

One of the reporters, a plump fellow with a name tag that identified him as JIM IVEY, ORLANDO SENTINEL, asked, "Is it true you're playing bit parts now, Groucho?"

"Actually, two-bit parts" he replied. "And it turns out they can't even afford me at that price."

"But were you really—a comic actor of your ability—seriously considering doing a shabby walk-on in one of Warlock's cheesy jungle fiascoes?"

Groucho looked from the questioning reporter to the young publicity man. "You actually paid to have this fellow shipped out here from Florida?"

The only woman reporter, labeled MADDY HAMBRICK, ST. LOUIS POST-DISPATCH, asked Groucho, "Is it true you've stopped making Marx Brothers movies?"

"You've probably heard, dear lady," he replied, "even in far-off St. Louis, of the Flying Dutchman. As it happens, Chico, Harpo, and I are sailing under a similar curse and must make Marx Brothers movies for the rest of our natural lives. Or in Chico's case, for the rest of his unnatural life. Only the kiss of a good woman can, in my case, break the spell. And just try to find a good woman in Hollywood. And as for a St. Louis woman with her diamond rings, wellsir—"

"Been great chatting with you, Grouch," said Mark Glidden. "No we've really got to hustle over to the *Hitler's Spy* set."

"Then this is farewell." Groucho stepped aside, after a slight bow, to let the reporters hurry on.

"Nice to have met you, Mr. Marx," called Maddy Hambrick.

"With all the nitwits already in Hollywood," Groucho said to himself, "it doesn't make sense to import more of them from out of town."

Twenty

Pushing open the door designated SECURITY DEPARTMENT, Groucho found himself in a small reception room. The walls were oak paneled, and at the metal desk sat a plump brunette young woman who was scowling at her typewriter.

Groucho went loping across the thick gray carpeting to snatch up the receptionist's left hand. Bending low, he delivered a smacking kiss and declared, "Gertie, it's so delightful to be in your presence once again."

"My name is Judy McRae, Mr. Marx," she informed him as she reclaimed her hand.

"Ah, forgive me, dear lady," he apologized, straightening up. "I mistook you for Gertrude Ederle, the noted Channel swimmer. That's probably due to the fact that you're wearing water wings, albeit in front. Still, the resemblance is quite—"

"You're a very silly man," she told him, giggling.

"Why, thank you," he said. "That's the kindest thing anyone's said to me since . . . well, come to think of it, it's the first kind thing anyone's *ever* said to me."

Lowering her voice, the receptionist confided, "Mr. Stone is expecting you. Be careful, he's in a sour mood."

"What prompted that?"

"Nothing, he's always in a sour mood." She picked up her desk phone. "Mr. Marx is here to see you, Mr. Stone."

Sour noise came out of the receiver.

Smiling, she pointed a thumb at the door behind her desk. "Good luck."

On the frosted-glass top portion of the door was inscribed in gold HURFORD E. STONE, PRIVATE.

Without knocking, Groucho entered. "Sorry to hear you're still a private, Stone old fellow," he said. "One would've thought you'd be at least a corporal by now."

Stone was a small man with thinning gray hair, in his middle fifties. Removing his pince-nez glasses, he glowered at Groucho. "I have never been an admirer of the Marx Brothers," he announced by way of greeting.

"I don't much care for them myself, but I've had a devil of a time trying to ditch them," Groucho said. "At least now I only have to work with two of them."

"Joel Farber informed me, in no uncertain terms, that I had to cooperate with you." Replacing his spectacles on his sharp, narrow nose, he, carefully, picked up the two sheets of yellow paper that were lying atop his gray desk blotter. "Allow me to say, Groucho, that I believe it's foolhardy not to rely solely on the police investigation of the unfortunate death of the late Randolph Spellman."

"And me, I'd replace you with an inexpensive calculating machine," said Groucho cordially. "But, alas, we have to take the world as we find it. And come winter, we have to take a large dose of sulfur and molasses."

Stone coughed into his small, well-manicured hand. "I was given a list of names by Mr. Farber," he said, "and ordered to determine if any of them had visited the Warlock grounds on the day of Randolph Spellman's demise."

"And did any of them? And if so, when did they arrive and depart?"

"Only two," answered Stone. "The actress Rochelle Shaye arrived at 10:44 A.M. on the day in question, coming by taxi. She had a scheduled appointment with Peter Maresca, one of our Warlock directors, and after visiting him on the set of *The Girl from Pawtucket* and dining in the directors' wing of the Warlock Commissary, she left the studio at 4:10 with Maresca in his Rolls Royce." He handed one of the yellow sheets to Groucho. "You may keep this for your files."

Groucho accepted it. "And the other visitor?"

"A Mr. Val Gallardo was admitted at 12:50 P.M.," continued Stone. "He was visiting the actor George Raft, who's here on loan from Warner Bros. to star in *1001 Nights in Sing Sing.* Gallardo left in his Pontiac at 6:14." He passed this yellow sheet across. "That's the lot, Groucho. Now I really must return to more-serious work."

"I appreciate your able assistance." Folding away the information, Groucho headed for the door.

Stone asked, "Is it true that the Marx Brothers are leaving the movies?"

"Would that we could," Groucho said, hand on the door handle. "But, alas, we were trapped into having to make two more alleged comedies for MGM. Look on the bright side, though, Stone. You may not live long enough to see that happen."

He left the office, paused to kiss Judy McRae's plump hand

once more and observe, "He's sour indeed," and then went striding manfully out into the sunlight.

The dilapidated dummy in the tattered tux looked even more forlorn, sprawled limply in his wicker armchair on the porch of the Westwood cottage where Dorothy Woodrow had been hiding out.

Enery opened the door before I reached it. "She's not here."

"No idea where she went?" I crossed the threshold.

He shook his head, answering, "There's no note and no sign of trouble."

"Could the police have found her?" We went into the parlor.

"If the cops busted in here, they sure as hell were neat about it."

"I can check with my Studio City police contact." I sat on the arm of one of the chairs. "Any idea how long she's been gone?"

Enery sank down onto the sofa. "We had dinner here together last night," he said. "I had a rehearsal for a play I'm doing over in Pasadena. When I got back here a little after midnight . . . shit, Dorothy wasn't here."

"Has that happened before?"

"For an hour or so maybe. If she thought it was safe, at night always, she'd take a careful walk around Westwood," my actor friend answered. "She's, you know, an athlete, and she gets restless cooped up."

"That's obviously not what she did last night."

"If it is, then something happened to her while she was out," Enery said, clenching his fist. "After waiting around for an hour, I went out myself. Took the route Dorothy usually takes. Nothing, no sign of her. I called the couple of her friends I can trust, and they hadn't heard from her. So then, Frank, I just sat around here and hoped she'd call. Toward dawn I dozed off for a few hours."

"It's possible she turned herself in."

"She'd have told me if she was planning anything like that."

"Was she thinking she ought to move someplace else to hide?"

"She never said anything about it."

I noticed that the golden-haired moppet dummy in the gingham dress was no longer sitting on the sofa. "Did you move the dummy?"

Enery gave me a puzzled look. "Huh?"

I pointed. "Blonde dummy's gone. You put it someplace else?"

"I didn't, no. Why?"

"Has her ventriloquist pal—Arnie Carr, isn't it? Has he been back?"

"No, Arnie's still up in Santa Francesca," Enery answered. "That Fiesta Week Festival is still going on."

"Let's look around for that dummy."

We went over the whole cottage, but found no trace of it.

In the bedroom Enery spotted something. "One of her suitcases is gone. I didn't notice that before."

"So if Arnie Carr telephoned her and asked her to bring him the dummy to use in his show," I asked, "would Dorothy have done it?"

"She would've told me, Frank."

"Still, she might've headed up there."

"Maybe, but—"

"Where's Carr staying?"

"At the Francesca Mission Inn. He's playing a week at the

restaurant attached to the inn, and they threw in a room." Slowly, Enery shook his head. "Dorothy wouldn't have headed up there without leaving a note."

I didn't mention that maybe she was switching boyfriends again. "Santa Francesca's only about an hour's drive up the coast," I said. "I can head up there and look around."

"I ought to go along with you," he said. "Except we're shooting a couple more cannibal scenes at Warlock this afternoon."

"I'll see if I can find any trace of her," I told him.

On my way to the Coast Highway, I stopped at a Rexall drugstore on Sunset. While walking through the place en route to the row of telephone booths at the rear, I passed the newsstand. The new issue of *Radio Mirror* had a nice color shot of Maggie Thompson, who played Hollywood Molly on our radio show, on the cover.

A ten-year-old kid wearing a beanie profusely decorated with old union buttons was perusing a copy of *Ty-Gor Comics* and his beanie-less buddy was arguing, "Tarzan is tougher than Ty-Gor. And Batman is tougher than both of them."

I deposited my nickel and asked the operator for my number.

"Jane Danner Studio," answered Myra.

"Didn't this used to be the Frank Denby Shrine?"

"Oh, hello, Mr. Denby. Want to talk to your wife?"

"Unless she's resting."

"No, she's penciling a daily. Hold on."

Jane said, "Is that honky-tonk music I hear in the background?"

"No, it's noise from the crowd fighting to get their hands on copies of *Radio Mirror*," I said. "Listen, Jane, I have to run an errand. It'll take around three hours or so."

"She's gone?"

"Yep, but I have a notion where she went."

"Not someplace where you're going to get conked on the head?"

"I know I've been knocked unconscious during just about all the cases Groucho and I have worked on thus far, darling, but this time—"

"*All* the darn cases. And sometimes *twice* per case."

"This trip doesn't involve any risk of head injuries," I assured her. "Are you all right?"

"I am, yes," she answered. "And I'll be fine when next we meet."

"Keep in mind that I love you. Bye."

Next I called the Studio City Police Department and asked for Detective Mitch Tandofsky.

He happened to be there. "Have you guys found out anything important, Frank?"

"Not yet," I admitted. "How about you?"

"Still working on the Spellman case."

I asked, casually, "Any news about Dorothy Woodrow?"

"We haven't located the lady," my detective friend told me. "Do you and Groucho know where she might be?"

"Nope." And this time I wasn't exactly lying.

"Turns out your actor pal Enery McBride had been keeping company with Dorothy," Tandofsky said. "He tell you about that?"

"Yeah, but he doesn't know where she is either."

"And she didn't confide in him that she was planning to bump off Randy Spellman?"

"You don't think she did, so why—"

"Never mind, I'll be talking to McBride on my next visit to Warlock."

"Anything you'd like to pass along?"

"Nothing, Frank. And you?"

"Nothing, Mitch."

"Well, let's keep exchanging information like this. Say hello to Jane." He hung up.

I left the booth and stopped again at the newsstand. I decided to pick up a copy of *Radio Mirror.*

The kid in the beanie was saying to his pal, "Superman's tougher than Batman and Tarzan *and* Ty-Gor."

Twenty-one

As Groucho slouched in a dignified manner toward the entrance of his office building, a thin woman in a cloth coat thrust an eleven-year-old boy into his path.

Groucho came to a stop, eyebrows elevating.

"Go ahead, Stanley," urged the bespectacled boy's mother.

Stanley wrinkled his nose. "But Ma, I don't want Groucho Marx."

"Few people, outside of a few rural sheriffs, do," Groucho said.

"Stanley's already got Ginger Rogers, Lew Ayres, and Lyle Talbot," said the woman.

"My advice is to hold them for ransom," advised Groucho. "Lyle Talbot isn't worth much, but Ginger Rogers should bring a pretty penny. Now, I don't know if you've seen the new pretty pennies, but they're the ones that depict Abraham Lincoln dressed as Scarlett O'Hara."

"Stanley would very much like your autograph for his collection, Mr. Marx."

"Aw, Ma, do I have to?"

"It'll be a wonderful souvenir of our visit to Hollywood."

"Nobody in East Moline gives a darn about Groucho Marx."

"You can inform them in East Moline, wherever it may be at the moment, that I don't give a darn about them. So there."

"Hand him your autograph album, Stanley."

"Okay, if you say so." He thrust a ragged blue album at Groucho.

After scrawling his name, Groucho patted the lad on the head in a kindly way. "Bless you, my lad," he said as the boy winced.

With the grace of a Fairbanks, so he later told me, Groucho went bounding up the stairway. "Nanette," he exclaimed as he burst into the outer office, "I am definitely a public idol and a darling of the masses. Fans are flocking to me like . . . like some kind of birds that are known for their flocking."

"It won't last," said his secretary. "Someday you'll be as obscure as Ramon Navarro."

"Who?"

"See what I mean?"

He headed for the door of his private office. "Once I'm snugly installed in there, with my favorite pipe and shawl," he instructed, "ring up Zeppo and tell him his favorite sibling wants to talk to him."

"The last time I told him that, he got awfully mad when he found out it wasn't Harpo."

"Be that as it may." Groucho entered his office.

A moment later his desk phone rang. "Black Hole of Calcutta, Reservations Desk," he answered. "What do you mean flippant, Zeppo? You don't expect a chap of my jolly nature to greet his beloved youngest brother with some trite greeting like, 'Howdy, Herbert,' or 'What's cooking?,' or . . . No, I'm not calling you simply to get some free information pertaining to the Spellman murder case that I happen . . . of course I'm interested in how you're feeling. Stick out your tongue and say, 'Ah.' Now, then . . . I promise not to mention the late Randy Spellman at all. . . . Well, perhaps the newspapers exaggerated my . . . I am moderately interested in . . . you ought to wait, Zep, and get your information from the horse's mouth or at least some part of the horse. No, I do enjoy chatting with you when I don't have an ulterior motive. . . . Well, maybe I have an interior motive, since I have this dreadful pain right about here, but . . . I haven't said you're not a brilliant conversationalist, and I will say that if I can get a word in edgewise. Although the last time we tried to insert a word in Edgewise, he made such an unholy fuss. . . . No, truly, Zeppo, you are known far and wide as a witty fellow. Indeed, some hint you're as witty as I am, but most of them are the same people who believe in Santa Claus, the Easter Bunny, and Orson Welles. . . . In fact, you're as droll as Oscar Wilde. Now then . . . No, I'm not accusing you of being a sissy. At any rate . . . I *am* getting to the point. There are a couple of tidbits of information I hope you can provide. I can only tell you that the fate of a nation may well hang in the balance. . . . What nation? Well, I think it's Albania, though it might be that little purple nation on page 43 of the Atlas we used to . . . Every time I try to have a cozy familial chat with you . . . Very well, I'd like to know something about an actress that I think you know, even though you don't represent her. Her name is Laura Dayton, and I'll be ever so grateful if you can find out where the lady was on the night that Spellman expired amidst the foliage. . . . How's that again? She was with you? With you and about sixty other people . . . at a cocktail party at Carole Lombard's. . . . What time was the . . . She was there from six in the evening until nearly eleven? And that included dinner and music by Warren Sattler and His Spurious Hawaiians? Well, that's a load off my mind, and if you know my mind, you're aware it isn't up to heavy lifting. . . . And I promise, Zeppo, I'll telephone you again soon and we'll do nothing but talk about the old days. The two old days we'll be discussing are Tuesday and Friday, so bone up. Farewell." He hung up.

They were dancing in the streets of Santa Francesca. I'd parked my Chevrolet in an impromptu parking lot that was taking advantage of the festivities to charge a whole buck for the privilege. It was five blocks from Main Street.

Walking in that direction, I began to hear music from guitars, drums, and tambourines. When I reached Mission Boulevard, I encountered a full-fledged parade. A platoon of dark-haired young ladies was dancing by. Wearing lacy mantillas and white dresses rich with lace, they were clicking castanets and stomping their feet frequently on the bright afternoon street.

Strung across the street from lamppost to lamppost was a large canvas banner proclaiming in red and green, FIESTA WEEK! On both sides of the wide street were two rows of watchers—local citizens and tourists.

Marching in the wake of the dancers were several bands. The first bunch, clad in much-embroidered *charro* outfits and wearing bright white sombreros, was playing guitars, mandolins, and what looked to me, if such a thing exists, like a portable marimba. The second band consisted of about two dozen Boy Scouts. In addition to their uniforms, they were wearing many-colored serapes. After a few more assorted groups of musicians, sixteen handsome white stallions came prancing. They had jewel-encrusted silver bridles and ornately carved leather saddles. The riders, a few of them on the plump side, possessed real moustaches of an elegance and size that would've made Groucho envious. They wore the sort of costumes that the Cisco Kid might have had his tailor whip up if he'd won the Irish Sweepstakes.

Bystanders on both sides of the broad boulevard were clapping, calling encouragement in both English and Spanish, waving American flags, Mexican flags, and, in one instance, a USC pennant.

Somewhere on the far side of the mounted riders, a string of firecrackers started popping. The sudden noise spooked one of the front-row horses. He whinnied, rose up, and went lurching toward the crowd across the way. Jerking on the silver-studded reins, the rider lost his bright sombrero, which spun into the parade watchers.

The white hat smacked into the chest of a fat man wearing a Hawaiian shirt and a camera. He reacted by dodging to his left and into the young woman standing next to him.

Even though she was wearing dark glasses and a gray scarf over her blonde hair, I recognized Dorothy Woodrow.

I started working my way toward the corner, nearly tripping over a short, squat woman who was standing on an orange crate, the better to view the passing parade.

The hatless caballero got his mount under control, the company of stallions moved on. In the gap between the last of the white horses and a massive crepe-paper float depicting the founding and development of California, I managed to sprint to the other side of Mission Boulevard.

Dorothy, by the time I got there, was no longer standing next to the fat man who'd been hit with the flying sombrero.

Hopping up onto a milk crate that had been abandoned, I scanned the crowd in both directions. I caught a glimpse of her

155

half a block to my left. She was hurrying away at the edge of the parade watchers.

I was pretty sure she hadn't seen me, since that immense load of crepe paper had shielded my dash to her side of the boulevard. I started following her. Dorothy had no reason, far as I knew, to avoid me, but I decided not to call out to her. Curious, I figured to tail her and find out just where she was going.

That turned out to be a mistake.

Twenty-two

Midway along the side street that Dorothy was hurrying down sat a parade float. It consisted of a replica of Mission Santa Francesca, built chiefly of flowers. The tile roofs were made of big red roses. Somebody had left it parked in front of a narrow yellow-front saloon called EL CAMINO CANTINA.

I slowed, keeping distance and wandering pedestrians between me and the fugitive stuntwoman. At the corner she turned to the right. I sprinted ahead, and as I passed the deserted float, a small shower of yellow rose petals fell free, scattering in my path.

By the time I reached the corner, Dorothy was cutting across a cobbled street toward the walled courtyard of the actual Mission Santa Francesca. Compared to all the other southern California buildings built in the mission style, Santa Francesca looked somewhat worn and shabby. Its high, thick adobe walls were thick with moss, some of it brown and dying.

Dorothy's advent into the courtyard caused several mourning doves to go flying up off the mossy flagstones surrounding a venerable fountain. I watched, unobtrusively I was sure, from the arched entryway, and I saw her open the heavy carved door of a small chapel that formed a sort of annex to the mission itself.

The few doves that had returned to peck at the scatter of bird seed someone had left alongside the fountain went fluttering away again when I made my careful way across the sunny courtyard.

I stopped at the door to the chapel, listening. The carving, I noticed, depicted Christ praying in the Garden of Gethsemane. I couldn't hear a thing through the thick wood. Reaching out, I took hold of the dark, timeworn metal latch.

Something extremely hard whapped me across the back of my neck. Lurching forward, I dealt the door a substantial thump with my forehead.

I tried to turn to see who'd hit me, but instead I crumpled to my knees. I was sapped again, hard, across the temple.

Collapsing to the flagstones and sinking into oblivion, my last thought was, *Damn, I promised Jane this wouldn't happen.*

The sun was shining brightly on Rodeo Drive. Groucho, quietly whistling "Lydia the Tattooed Lady," was wending his way along a row of currently fashionable Beverly Hills shops and restaurants. When he came to a lingerie shop called Françoise, Groucho ceased whistling and entered. A tiny bell tinkled.

A thickset man in a blue double-breasted suit and a very red tie was holding a black latex girdle out in front of him, discussing the garment with a pretty blonde clerk who stood behind the highly polished darkwood counter. "I'm undecided," he was saying.

"This one is extremely popular just now, Mr. Silverlake," the young woman told him in a barely believable French accent.

Noticing Groucho, the hefty accountant waggled the girdle,

causing the garters to flap. "How do you think Corky will look in this, Groucho?"

"Thinner."

"No, seriously now."

"Who or what is Corky?" Groucho moved closer to Ira Silverlake.

"I thought I introduced her to you at that party at Zanuck's last month."

"No, that was my night to bowl with the fellows from the plant, and I missed the party," replied Groucho. "Could we, perhaps, chat a bit about Doug Cahan?"

Silverlake frowned at his platinum wristwatch. "This is a busy week for me, Groucho, since I'm just back from San Diego," he explained. "That's why I asked you to meet me here. Kill two birds with one stone, as it were."

"You know, Ira, I've never been able to do that," admitted Groucho. "Though once in Ireland I killed two snakes with one scone."

"I think I'll take this." Silverlake handed the garment to the young clerk. "Gift wrap it and have it sent to Miss LaViolet. And stick in the usual message."

" 'To my dearest one' again?"

He asked Groucho, "Does that sound too flowery?"

"Not for someone named Corky LaViolet, no sir," he said. "Can we go someplace and talk about Doug Cahan?"

The accountant had started writing a check. "Thanks so much for your help, Delphine," he said, sliding the check across the glass top of the counter.

"A pleasure, as always, monsieur."

Silverlake, taking hold of Groucho's arm, led him over to a love seat that faced a counter display of three manikin torsos wearing frilly bras. He sat down, saying, "If you ask me, Groucho, Doug got a raw deal. The kid was framed, I'm damned certain."

"By whom?" Groucho seated himself as far from the bulky man as the narrow chair would allow.

"One of those bastards out at Arthur Wright Benson, Inc.," he answered. "Doug wasn't the kind of kid who'd tap the till. He worked for me for nearly four years, and he was honest."

"Okay," said Groucho, glancing at the laciest brassiere, "if Cahan was honest, trustworthy, reverent, and brave and didn't swipe any dough—why'd he run away?"

"I think Doug, once he realized they were trying to set him up for an embezzling rap, took off for the tall grass," said Silverlake. "He wasn't all that happy, last time I talked to him, about the whole setup out at Rancho Tygoro."

"For instance?"

"Alicia Benson, for instance."

"The lad was supposed to be engaged to Benson's daughter."

"He was, more or less. I only met her once, at a party at Selznick's, but from the hints Doug dropped, I'd say she was a very possessive young lady. He'd been thinking about breaking off the whole damn relationship, but was afraid it might cost him his job. And old Benson paid well."

Groucho nodded. "And what other problems did he encounter in that tropical paradise?"

"You know the son? A first-class *putz* and a champion kvetcher," said Silverlake. "Didn't think Doug was much of an accountant and told him so. Also told him Alicia deserved a lot better than him." He stood up. "Afraid that's all I can tell you. Doug was a good kid, and I trusted him. He didn't steal anything. Now I've got to get back to the old grind."

Rising, Groucho asked, "You haven't heard from Cahan?"

Shaking his head, Silverlake headed for the door. "Not a word, Groucho, but I figure that's because he's lying low for a while." He stepped out onto Rodeo Drive. "You ought to talk to his sister. She might know something."

"Where might I find the lass?"

"Last time I heard, which was a couple months back when I ran into her at a party at the Rathbones', she was singing at a nightspot down on the beach in Santa Monica," he answered. "She calls herself Kitty Kahane. She's some kind of jazz singer. Myself, I don't understand swing, and if it's not Guy Lombardo, I leave music alone."

"What's the name of the nightspot?"

Silverlake thought. "Oh, yeah, it's called the Mermaid Tavern," he told Groucho. "How does Doug Cahan, by the way, tie in with Randy Spellman's murder?"

"Possibly not at all," answered Groucho. "But I have a hunch he might. Before I had a hunch, I had a rash, and, let me tell you, this is much less painful."

Twenty-three

The smell of incense was strong, and my head ached.

"Often we tend to overindulge during fiesta time," someone was saying in a soft, understanding voice.

I found myself seated in a wooden pew at the rear of the small, shadowy chapel. Up near the narrow altar several red rows of votive candles were flickering. Watching the flames flickering seemed to increase my head pains.

Watching me from the aisle was a dark-haired priest in a long black cassock. A string of wooden rosary beads was wound around his weathered right hand.

After making certain I was still capable of breathing in and out, I said, "Strange as it may seem, Father, I haven't been drinking."

"You needn't explain your sorry condition, son."

When I attempted to rise, the pale orange adobe walls started to wobble. Closing my eyes for a moment, I tottered into the aisle.

The priest steadied me with his left hand. "You've been hurt," he noticed now.

Gingerly, I touched at my temple. It felt sticky, and my fingers came away smeared with drying blood. "I must've fallen."

"Perhaps you need medical—"

"No, that's okay. I'll be fine." My proclamation would have been more convincing had I not made such a staggering exit.

The brightness of the sun outside seemed to have doubled in intensity. I meant to exhale, but it came out more like a grunt.

The soft-spoken priest advised, "I wouldn't drink anymore today."

"I intend to quit for life." It took me a while to cross the courtyard and reach the street. This time the doves didn't stir, probably realizing that I was at present no threat to them.

By the time I'd walked to the Francesca Mission Inn, which lay three blocks from the scene of my conking, I was no longer wobbly. My headache continued, and my pace was slower, but I felt I was, slowly, recovering.

It bothered me that I was apparently the sort of person who attracted blows to the skull. I'd been hoping, now that fatherhood was so near, that being knocked silly was a thing of the past.

The hotel was built in a modified Spanish style. The main building, three stories high, had slanting red-tile roofs, a bright white-stucco façade dotted with many grilled windows. There were high hedges and tall palm trees, arched doorways and mosaic-tile paths.

The large oval lobby was floored with colored tiles, ringed with potted palms. The air-conditioning was on too high. Holding my hand so that it, unobtrusively, covered my bonked head, I made my way to the rest rooms. A sign on the left-hand redwood portal announced, HOMBRES. I went in.

"Yikes," I remarked upon seeing myself in the mirror over the sink.

There were an ugly smear of dried blood on my cheek and more darkened blood matting the hair over my ear. Turning on the faucet, I fished out my handkerchief, dampened it, and, wincing frequently, cleaned off the spot where I'd been slugged.

Looking somewhat more presentable, I returned to the lobby and made my way to a table that offered envelopes, stationery, and postcards for the guests of the inn. I wrote Arnie Carr's name on an envelope, folded in a sheet of blank paper, and crossed to the desk.

Because of the fiesta, the desk clerk was wearing a sombrero. "Good afternoon, sir," he said as I stopped in front of the registration counter. "My, looks like you've had a bit of an accident."

"I'm afraid my fiery Irish temper has gotten me into trouble once again," I explained, handing across the envelope. "I'd like to leave this message for Arnie Carr."

The tassels on his sombrero jiggled as the pudgy young man turned to glance at the rows of pigeonholes behind him. "His key's in, meaning he's out. I'll pop this in his box for you." He took the spurious letter.

Turning, he slipped it into a box that had BUNG. 3 printed beneath it.

"Gracias," I said, getting into the spirit of things.

To the right of the inn's main building was a row of a dozen or so bungalows. Red-tile roofs, white stucco walls, brass numbers on their redwood doors. I'd noticed them when I arrived.

Bungalow 3 had a blue 1937 Plymouth coupe parked in the space next to it. Sitting in the open rumble seat was a ventriloquist dummy I hadn't encountered before—a weak-chinned cowboy.

165

Walking up to the door of the bungalow, I knocked. There was no response. I knocked again.

Then, after making certain that there was nobody in the vicinity, I picked the lock and went inside.

The shadowy living room smelled of old cigarettes and pungent furniture polish. The door to the bathroom was partially open, and you could hear a faucet persistently dripping.

The blonde female ventriloquist dummy that had disappeared from the Westwood apartment was sitting stiffly in a redwood chair, seemingly staring in the direction of a large brown radio that squatted between the unmade twin beds. The radio was one of those where you had to insert a quarter to make it play for a few hours. I wondered if anybody had parted with two bits to hear our *Hollywood Molly* radio show.

Against the wall rested a suitcase that matched the ones Dorothy had left behind.

Patting the dummy on her head, I started searching the room. Taped to the underside of the only drawer in the small writing desk. I found a grey envelope.

It contained six photographs, different from the ones we'd found in Randy Spellman's black box. I recognized several of the people in this batch of compromising positions. There was also a crudely drawn copy of the crudely drawn map, the one that probably showed where something was buried.

Sighing, I put all the stuff back and reaffixed the envelope where I'd found it.

I was on my knees again, picking the lock on Dorothy's suitcase, when the door of the motel room opened slowly.

Rising and turning, I saw Dorothy coming in out of the bright afternoon. She was holding a .32 revolver.

Twenty-four

When Groucho parked his Cadillac near the beach in Santa Monica, a light mist was starting to drift in over the Pacific. It swirled around him, as he emerged from the car, smelling faintly of seaweed.

He heard the Mermaid Tavern before he saw it. A polite-sounding jazz music came drifting in his direction. A small group was playing "Blue Moon," with a Benny Goodman–like clarinet taking the lead.

The club sat between a white-fronted seafood restaurant and a real estate office. The tavern was narrow, with a peach-colored stucco façade and a hanging wooden sign depicting a rather chubby smiling mermaid.

Taking one more breath of sea air, Groucho entered the dim-lit club.

Up on the small bandstand a slim brunette in slacks and a ribbed pullover was singing the lyrics to the Rogers and Hart tune and improvising with a little scat singing.

A poster-board sign resting on an easel just inside the door announced, EVERY NIGHT BUT TUESDAY . . . WALT NEEDHAM & HIS SO-PHISTICATED SWING SEXTET. WITH THE DELIGHTFUL KITTY KAHANE.

Except for the group on the bandstand and a waiter who was taking the upended chairs down off the tables, the Mermaid Tavern was empty.

Noticing Groucho, the clarinetist stopped playing. "Hey, you're Groucho Marx."

"Yes, but I came to Santa Monica to try to forget that." He approached the bandstand. "It seemed cheaper than joining the Foreign Legion."

The young singer said, "We're just about finished rehearsing, Mr. Marx. I can talk with you in about five minutes. Okay?"

"Play on," Groucho ordained, seating himself at one of the small, round tables.

The short, wide waiter came over, grinning. "Do you know what my favorite Marx Brothers movie is?"

"*Gone with the Wind*?"

"That's not a Marx Brothers movie."

"It isn't? Well then, no wonder Clark Gable got so testy every time I tried to carry Vivien Leigh up that staircase."

"*Duck Soup,*" said the persistent waiter.

"No, thanks, I just had lunch."

"*Duck Soup* is the funniest film you boys ever made, Mr. Marx."

"That's because Zeppo was in it," Groucho explained. "And he's a barrel of laughs. He used to be a barrel of monkeys, but he discovered, despite rumors to the contrary, that that was no fun."

"Well, keep up the good work." The waiter returned to getting the place ready for the evening customers.

The sextet finished up a swing arrangement of "Isn't It Romantic?," and, gathering up their instruments, drifted away into the shadows.

Kitty Kahane came down the bandstand steps to join Groucho. "Would you like a drink, Mr. Marx? I can—"

"Not unless your tavern stocks celery tonic, no."

"Okay, then let's talk about my brother." She rested her clasped hands on the table. "As I told you on the telephone, Doug's not a crook. He didn't steal one penny from those damned Bensons."

"Do you know where he is?"

Sighing and shaking her head, she answered, "No, Mr. Marx. I haven't heard from Doug since he disappeared. I'm worried, especially after all this time, that something's happened to him. That he had an accident or that somebody hurt him. Right after he went missing, I got a private detective who's a friend of Walt Needham's to try to track Doug down. But after a week he gave up."

Nodding, Groucho asked, "Do you have any idea why they'd try to frame him for stealing the money from Arthur Wright Benson, Inc.?"

"Sure, my bet is it was that bitch."

"Narrow that down a bit."

"Alicia Benson is the bitch I mean," explained the missing accountant's sister. "She and Doug had a . . . well, I guess you could call it a romance. But she was a very moody dame, and she could be nasty. He'd pretty much made up his mind to call it quits."

"How close to that was the time he'd disappeared?"

"Two, three weeks," Cahan's sister replied. "I told Doug, from the first time I met Alicia, that she looked like she could be a pain in the backside. But for a while, poor guy, he was really head over heels over her."

Groucho asked, "Did you know Randy Spellman?"

"The actor who got shot?" She shook her head. "No, but it sounds like he's another victim of the Ty-Gor jinx, doesn't it? First my brother gets framed and disappears, then this Muscle Beach type gets killed."

"Spellman never tried to contact you?"

A puzzled frown touched her forehead. "No, why the heck should he?"

"Apparently he didn't have any reason." Groucho stood up, giving the singer his office phone number. "If you should hear from your brother, let me know."

She said, "I have a feeling, Mr. Marx, that I'm not going to hear from him."

The first thing Dorothy Woodrow said was, "I'm sorry you got hit on the head, Frank. Are you okay?"

I looked from the revolver to her face and then back to the revolver. "Fine, I'm getting used to being rendered unconscious," I told her. "Who hit me?"

"Oh, that was Arnie. He made a mistake."

"Who was he supposed to slug?"

"He thought you were some kind of cop tailing me." She came farther into the room, closing the door behind her. "He got worried when I was late getting back, and came looking for me. That's how he spotted you following me."

"And why'd you go to the mission?"

"I'd stopped in at the chapel to say a prayer and light a candle. I used to be a Catholic, and it's a hard habit to break."

"Do you carry that gun when you go to church?"

She slipped the revolver into her purse. "I wasn't sure who was in here. I heard somebody moving around."

"What exactly," I inquired, "is going on?"

Dorothy sat on the edge of one of the rumpled beds, took a pack of cigarettes out of her purse. "There were some things I had to take care of," she said. She drew a cigarette out of the pack and lit it. "And I don't want to give myself up until the police find out who really murdered Randy."

"Or until Groucho and I find out?"

She smiled very briefly. "Sorry, but I don't have as much faith in you guys as Enery does," she told me. "Have you found out anything?"

"Quite a lot, but not who did it," I answered. "You sure it wasn't actually you?"

"I didn't kill him, no."

I was leaning back against the wall now. "Why'd you leave Westwood?"

"I had some things to take care of."

"You ought to have told Enery. He's been—"

"Enery's getting himself way too involved in my troubles," Dorothy said, sighing out smoke. "That can only screw up his life and his career, Frank."

"You've moved on," I suggested.

She took a slow drag on the cigarette, shrugging casually. "Yeah, that might be part of it," she admitted. "You've probably heard things about me, and some of them are true. I'm not the kind of person who stays put long."

"Apparently Enery didn't know that."

"Look, I like Enery," she said. "But even if this rotten business hadn't happened, I would've . . . well, as you put it, moved on. That's the way I am. Sorry."

"And Arnie Carr?"

"We're good friends. Not lovers. Not anymore, anyway."

"Where is he at the moment?"

"He does an afternoon show at the club here."

"Why'd you bring him the dummy?"

"Arnie decided he wanted to add her to his act for the evening shows," Dorothy said. "So I brought her up to him. Plus which, that gave me a good excuse to get out of Westwood before the police located me."

"No other reason for coming to Santa Francesca?"

She eyed me, snuffing out the cigarette in an abalone-shell ashtray atop the pay-radio. "No, Frank."

"So you and Arnie aren't partners?"

"Partners in what?"

"Show business, anything." I had long since decided not to mention the stuff I'd found in the gray envelope.

"Nope."

"Any message for Enery?"

She located another cigarette and lit it. "Just tell him I'm okay," she said. "And that I'm sorry. I guess I should've left him a note."

"I'll tell him," I said, and left there.

Twenty-five

Jane's attitude combined sympathy and annoyance. "You'd think by now," she was saying as she applied antiseptic to my abrasions, "that you'd have developed some kind of sixth sense, Frank, and—"

"Ouch, that stings."

"Good. Some sixth sense that would warn you when somebody was sneaking up to conk you."

I executed a sort of embarrassed schoolboy shuffle on the tiles of the bathroom floor. "I know, and I'm chagrined about lacking a sixth sense," I said, wincing as my wife applied a bandage to the side of my head. "Fact is, I'm not all that sure I have the basic five senses."

Contemplating myself in the mirror over the sink, I decided I looked somewhat better than I had when I'd last taken inventory.

Closing the door to the medicine cabinet, Jane returned to our living room.

I followed, after one final look at myself, and settled down beside her on the sofa.

"How did Enery take the news?" Jane asked.

I'd already told her what I'd found when I searched Arnie

Carr's room at the Francesca Mission Inn and about my conversation with Dorothy. "I gave him a somewhat censored account," I said. "I didn't tell Enery about the blackmail stuff, softened Dorothy's reasons for departing from Westwood."

"In other words, you lied."

"I lied, yeah. Eventually I'll have to tell him about Dorothy," I said. "Right now, I don't think we know everything that's going on."

"What if she really did kill Spellman?"

"No, I don't think that's—"

Our doorbell rang.

Dorgan, who'd been slumbering noisily in Jane's studio, awoke and commenced barking.

Getting up, I crossed to the door.

Our bloodhound, tail wagging, came trotting behind me.

Groucho was on the doorstep. "Good evening, sir or madam," he said. "We're conducting a house-to-house survey in our neighborhood. The question is 'Who would you rather have at the door—the wolf or Groucho Marx?'"

"Can we get a look at the wolf?"

"Sorry, time's up, and you didn't win the Pulitzer Prize. Better luck next time." He came slouching in out of the night.

Groucho set his coffee cup on the end table beside his armchair. "This stuff, Rollo, is a distinct improvement over the last batch I endured under your roof," he said. "Your skill as a brewer is improving."

"Jane made the coffee this time," I confessed.

My wife asked him, "What do you think Dorothy is up to?"

I'd just filled him in on my experiences in Santa Francesca.

I tried to minimize my getting slugged, which was difficult with my head bandaged up.

Legs creaking a bit, Groucho arose to commence pacing our living room. "It strikes me as quite possible, kiddies, that the lady was either helping the late Ty-Gor with his blackmailing," he said, circling the sprawled Dorgan, "or she's contemplating taking over the business. Hence the additional incriminating snapshots and the copy of the map. And the voice-throwing Arnie Carr may become her new partner in crime."

"Looks possible, yeah," I agreed. "Though I still don't think she killed Spellman."

Groucho halted in mid-rug. "The Southern belle," he said, making a nearly successful attempt to snap his fingers.

"The one O'Hearn told me about and the woman Salermo told you contacted Gallardo?"

"That Southern belle, yes." Groucho resumed pacing. "Little Dot might well be the lass in question, since a *Gone with the Wind* accent is easy to fake. Shall I demonstrate that point?"

"No," Jane told him. "We take your word for it."

"If she was in cahoots with Randy Spellman," I pointed out, "then she lied to us about her reason for going to his trailer the night the guy was killed. He wasn't blackmailing her."

"True," Groucho agreed. "It's still possible, though, that she was lured there by some sort of phony missive. I still believe somebody wanted to frame her for the murder."

"Somebody who knew she was working with him," my wife said.

"Maybe a blackmail victim," I added.

Groucho's slouch increased the more he paced. "Thus far none of the Spellman victims we know about were anywhere near him at the time he was shot."

"Far as we know," I said.

Jane asked, "What did you find out about that Arthur Wright Benson, Inc., accountant who took off, Groucho?"

Returning to his chair, he recounted his interviews with Ira Silverlake and Doug Cahan's singing sister. "He's tied in with this some way," he concluded. "I'm not sure how, but I've got an uneasy feeling. It may just be that I need a dose of castor oil, yet I fancy not."

"His sister could be lying," suggested Jane, "and actually know where he's hiding."

Groucho shook his head. "I don't think so. Although there are recorded instances of my being fooled by women."

"Spellman might've known where this embezzler was hiding out," I said. "So either Cahan or his fiancée, Alicia Benson, would have a damn good reason to do him in."

"Alicia and Doug weren't lovebirds anymore, Rollo." Groucho drank some of his coffee. "According to reliable sources, the romance had cooled considerably before Cahan dropped from sight. Therefore, it seems unlikely they'd team up on anything, even murder."

"The map," Jane mentioned quietly.

"The map indeed, Lady Jane," said Groucho. "Spellman had a copy, *and* Dorothy and her ventriloquist chum had a copy. We have reason to believe it's a map of part of Benson's private jungle, and it's safe to assume that it's an important document and that something of value is buried there."

"You fellows ought to get out to Rancho Tygoro with a shovel and a compass," suggested Jane.

"That may be where Cahan buried his loot," I said.

"Or it may be," said my wife, "where somebody buried Cahan."

Twenty-six

Groucho and I stepped out of his Cadillac and into the growing night fog that was hanging over this stretch of the San Fernando Valley. We left the car parked at the edge of a wide stretch of what looked like pastureland. The road that quirked along the back side of Arthur Wright Benson's private jungle was deserted.

"This is an extremely heavy shovel," mentioned Groucho, who was carrying it. "When you suggested bringing one along, I envisioned one of those lightweight shovels that one takes to the beach along with a tin pail."

"Colorful, but not too good for long-term digging." I was hefting a canvas knapsack containing a couple of flashlights, my old Boy Scout compass, and a pastrami sandwich that Groucho had happened to have in his glove compartment.

The fog was chill, smelling of grass and cow manure.

On our right loomed up a high hurricane fence. "According to the fabled Spellman treasure map, the rear gate will pop up soon," said Groucho.

"And there aren't supposed to be any guards back here."

"Are you certain of that, Rollo? I'd hate to be shot in this rural setting," he said. "A headline like 'Marx Felled in Cow Pasture' doesn't have any zing. Come to think of it, I haven't had much zing myself since, oh, about the second year of the Coolidge administration."

"This afternoon I called somebody I know in the local sheriff's office. Told him I was researching an article on the Benson jungle, and I just happened to ask about the guard setup," I explained. "There's the gate."

Set in the thick wire fence was a sturdy metal gate.

Putting down my knapsack, I fetched out my lock picks. The fog seemed to be closing in on us.

Groucho leaned on the handle of the shovel, striking a rustic pose, and watched me tinker with the lock. "I declare, Mr. Raffles, it's just so thrilling to see you at work," he said. "That, by the way, was a sample of the Scarlett O'Hara accent your missus forbade me from demonstrating earlier."

"I didn't know Scarlett O'Hara was Italian." Returning the picks to my pocket, I turned the handle. With a faint creak, the gate opened inward.

A narrow trail led into the dark, misty jungle. Tall trees rose up on each side, their tops lost in the fog. There were palm trees and trees I still couldn't identify, thick brush, hanging vines, tropical flowers. You could hear small creatures scurrying over dry leaves and fallen branches.

As I quietly shut the heavy gate, a louder thrashing and fluttering commenced on the right of us.

"Lions would make more noise than that, would they not?" inquired Groucho.

"Sure, and they'd probably roar."

"Ah, yes, much the way Leo does at the commencement of each and every MGM movie," said Groucho. "Did you know that when Leo is on vacation Louis B. Mayer used to stand in for him. MGM had to stop that, because women, children, and many weak-hearted men ran screaming in terror from motion picture palaces as soon as Mayer gave forth. If you've never experienced a Louis B. Mayer growl, you haven't—"

"Let's locate the pool." I found a flashlight in my knapsack, took the copy Jane had made of Spellman's map from my jacket pocket.

"Did your lawman chum have any details to pass along about the animal denizens of this jungle?" asked Groucho as we moved slowly along the mossy trail. "To be more specific, are there any large wild animals roaming loose?"

"No, nothing but assorted wild birds and a few tame monkeys."

"Small monkeys?"

"Tiny ones."

"Good, because ever since I was a wee infant, I've had an unnatural fear of large apes," he admitted. "For instance, the first time I met King Kong, at a cocktail party his studio threw for him, I nearly jumped out of my skin. My dermatologist later told me, considering the state of my epidermis, that jumping out of my skin wouldn't have been a bad idea." He stopped, glancing off to the left. "Did you hear a splash from over yonder?"

"Yeah, sounded like something just fell into . . . maybe a pond."

"Let us explore. Pass me a flashlight."

I took the other flash out of the knapsack, handed it to him. "This thing smells of pastrami."

"No respectable expedition is complete without a goodly supply of pastrami." Clicking on the light, he turned the beam on the jungle next to him. "Some explorers prefer liverwurst, but for me pastrami is the sandwich of choice. When my colleagues and I discovered King Tut's delicatessen, we carried . . . what ho, Franklin."

We'd been moving along between tall trees, and now we saw in a small clearing up ahead a pond that was about twenty yards in diameter. A large frog gave an indignant croak and leaped into the dark water, producing a gulping splash.

I circled the pond, moving to the far side. I took out my compass and a tape measure. After a moment I pointed and said, "If this is the body of water we want, we have to go in this direction to dig."

Using the metal tape measure, I measured out twenty-one feet. That brought us to a patch of ground in another small clearing amidst the high, thick trees.

"This could well be the spot," said Groucho, using the beam of his flash to point at the ground.

Over a large patch of ground, the moss was sparser and not as thick as the surrounding growth, and it was a slightly different shade of green.

"I do hate to be gloomy," said Groucho, "yet I can't help noticing that this plot of ground is about the size of an average grave."

"I was thinking that, too."

"Let us be up and digging." He handed me the shovel.

Rubbing his hands together, Groucho said, "Let me know when it's my turn with the shovel, Rollo." He was sitting on a fallen log, his back resting against a tree trunk.

I'd cleared away about two feet of earth from the suspected burial spot. "If we don't find something pretty quick, I'll . . . oops."

The tip of the shovel had struck something that wasn't dirt.

Laying the shovel down beside the newborn hole in the ground, I crouched and started scooping away earth with my hands.

Groucho got up, moving closer. Clicking his flashlight back on and shining it down. "That looks mighty like part of a blanket."

A section of a thick plaid blanket, much the worse for having been buried for some time, was showing through. It smelled of damp earth. And I was noticing the odor of something else.

As I rubbed more clumps of dirt away, my right hand tore off a section of the rotting cloth. "Jesus," I said, jerking back.

The remains of a hand showed through the rent in the plaid blanket.

"We seem to have found the missing accountant," observed Groucho in a very subdued voice.

In another twenty minutes or so, we had the bundled body up out of its lonesome grave.

While Groucho watched, I, a bit gingerly I admit, un-wrapped the makeshift shroud. From what was left of the dead man, it was possible to conclude that he was quite probably Doug Cahan. There were two bullet holes in the chest of the muddy white shirt he was wearing, ringed with blackened blots of long-dried blood.

After standing away from the corpse for a moment and tak-ing in a few breaths of misty air, I knelt again to make a search of what remained of the suit he was wearing. In a rotting breast pocket of the jacket, I found a black-leather wallet encrusted with splotches of dead-white mildew.

Behind a stained glassine panel was a California state driver's license. " 'Douglas Cahan,' " I read. " 'Must wear corrective lenses.' "

"His sister was right," said Groucho. "He never stole any money."

"Well, if he did steal any, he never got very far with it." Wrapping the dead man's wallet in my handkerchief, I slipped it into my coat pocket. "Now we have to get the hell out of this jungle and contact the nearest sheriff's substation."

"Indeed? I was planning to rush home and hide under the bed for a spell. But, yes, your suggestion is a better—"

That was as far as he got.

From off to our left came a rifle shot.

Twenty-seven

The slug smacked into the trunk of a tree about three feet from where Groucho was standing. By the time the second rifle shot came whistling out of the foggy darkness, I was stretched out on the damp ground next to the corpse of the no-longer-missing accountant. I'd also clicked off my flashlight.

"Are you still among the living?" Groucho inquired in a low voice. "I'm fairly certain I am."

"So far, yeah." Using my elbows to propel me, I made my way across the jungle floor to where he was crouching in the brush.

"Apparently they don't take kindly to grave robbers in these parts."

"This could be one of the guards," I said, "or somebody from the main house."

"Whoever it is, Rollo, I doubt they're in the mood to negotiate. Therefore an orderly retreat is called for."

"We can't go back the way we came, since our rifleman is between us and the trail to the rear gate."

"We'll go deeper into the foliage, try to circle back."

Crouched low, Groucho and I moved in among the thickness of trees that surrounded the extemporaneous grave site. We were hoping the thick fog would swallow us up and make us hard to find.

After less than a minute another shot was fired. This one tore through a stand of high ferns some five or six feet ahead of us.

"He's not giving up," I whispered as we kept moving deeper into the night jungle.

"This reminds me of an old RKO talkie entitled *The Most Dangerous Game*," observed Groucho in a low voice. "Only for that chase through the jungle, Joel McCrea had Fay Wray for a companion and not a callow screenwriter."

"That's funny, I thought that I was playing the Joel McCrea part, and I was about to complain about having a superannuated comedian for a companion instead of Fay Wray."

"Let's try a short cut." Groucho dodged to the right, easing between the boles of two massive trees.

A dangling vine slapped wetly across my face as I followed.

We cut a zigzag swatch through the jungle for a few quiet minutes.

Suddenly, up ahead, several frightened night birds went squawking and flapping up from the low branches of a tall tree.

About twenty seconds after that, we heard heavy footfalls from some distance behind us.

"Our would-be assassin's picked up our scent once again," remarked Groucho.

We changed course once more. I realized I'd long since lost any idea of what direction we were heading. Maybe I'd get a chance, eventually, to consult my venerable compass.

"This is nowhere near as much fun as tiptoeing through the tulips." observed Groucho after a moment.

I could no longer hear the sound of the fellow who was hunting us. But that didn't mean we were anywhere near being safe.

After another few minutes we reached another small clearing. Glancing up, I noticed, very blurred and fuzzy through the fog, a tree house built in the limbs of a sturdy tree. "Hey, this must be the hut Spellman indicated on his map."

"It might make a temporary hiding place."

"We'll give it a try." I sprinted across the sward, grabbed the end of the rope ladder that dangled down from the platform porch of the Ty-Gor tree house that had been installed here for the last movie. I held it tight. "You first, Groucho."

"The last ladder I climbed was on a fire escape," he said, starting to ascend. "That time I was coming *down* to avoid an unexpected husband."

I went up after him.

Groucho was squatting on the porch, catching his breath. "Too bad Maureen O'Sullivan isn't at home."

"Wrong jungle man series," I pointed out.

"Alas, so it is."

We went inside the two-room hut.

"I don't know if I want to sign a lease on this place or not," said Groucho, glancing around at the bamboo walls and the raw-wood furniture. "It's cozy enough, but there are far too many gunmen in the neighborhood."

"Wonder why Spellman mentioned this tree hut on his map!"

"Either he was planning to settle down amidst the palms, or he possibly hid something here."

185

"Until it's safe to emerge, let's, making no noise, look around."

"Yes, Rollo, that'll pass the time better than telling ghost stories around the campfire."

Beneath a straw mat in the second room was another gray envelope. Guardedly using my flash, I determined that it contained two more photos. These, however, didn't show romantic encounters but a burial.

Jack Benson was digging the grave we'd found near the pond. Lying beside it, still not enshrouded in the plaid blanket, was Doug Cahan's body. He was easily recognizable at that stage. Standing next to the corpse was Alicia Benson, and she was smiling.

"I believe," said Groucho, looking over my shoulder, "this is what sleuths from time immemorial have called a pretty kettle of fish."

"It gives the Bensons a terrific motive for killing Spellman," I said quietly. "Spellman spotted them getting rid of Cahan's body, took some infrared shots, and subsequently blackmailed Alicia."

"And she apparently shot the accountant when he informed her they were no longer an item," added Groucho. "After all, no self-respecting lass likes to be jilted. And a crazy, violent-tempered young lady like Alicia Benson is the type who shoots boyfriends who try to ditch her."

"That's likely what happened. When she got tired of paying blackmail to Spellman, she snuck onto the Warlock lot and shot him."

"More than likely smuggling herself in with that load of palm trees that was sent over from this very jungle in which we find ourselves cowering."

I whispered, "Quiet for a minute."

From the jungle below the tree hut came the sound of someone walking over fallen leaves. Walking slowly and carefully.

I automatically held my breath.

Two very long minutes passed.

The footsteps were growing fainter.

"I'd give a sigh of relief," said Groucho, "but I'm afraid he'd hear it."

We sat in silence for a good ten minutes more before deciding to leave the tree hut.

While up in the tree, I'd thought of another way to get ourselves out of this mess.

The fog followed us out of the jungle.

Moving through swirls of gray, Groucho and I began sneaking toward the Arthur Wright Benson, Inc., office building. There wasn't a single light showing inside.

Groucho, by exercising considerable willpower, refrained from saying anything while we approached the building.

I crouched at the front door, and, after trying the doorknob, I went to work on the lock with a couple of my picks. That took less than two minutes.

The heavy door opened inward with nary a sound. We slipped inside the building, and I eased the door shut.

Clicking on his flashlight, Groucho shined the beam on the corridor. "There ought to be a telephone in Benson's office," he concluded after illuminating the door of the nearest office.

The door of Arthur Wright Benson's executive office wasn't locked. We went in.

My flash located a phone sitting atop the large darkwood desk.

"Golly, I bet there are all sorts of lovely pictures of Ty-Gor decorating the walls," said Groucho. "If only we dared turn on the lights, I could feast my eyes. Or there might be an icebox full of sandwiches, and I could feast my—"

"I'll call my friend with the sheriff's office," I said, picking up the receiver. "And tell him we've found Doug Cahan."

Twenty-eight

We were heading for the office door when all the lights came blazing on.

"Trespassing is a serious offense," said Jack Benson, who was standing in the open doorway with a hunting rifle tucked under his right arm.

Groucho glanced slowly at the walls of the big office. "By Jove, I was dead right," he said. "Pictures of Ty-Gor in abundance. Though now that I give it some consideration, I probably shouldn't have used the phrase 'dead right.'"

There were several-dozen framed pictures of the jungle king on the buff-colored walls. Photos of assorted actors, book jackets, paintings, and drawings.

"In these parts," Arthur Wright Benson's son informed us, "it's the custom to shoot prowlers. I think we'll do that. Later we'll be tearful and apologetic about not recognizing you buffoons until it was too late. We'll be saddened, you'll be dead."

"You won't be able to bury us the way you did Doug Cahan," I pointed out.

"C'mon, shoot them, Jack." Alicia Benson, wearing dark

slacks and a navy blue windbreaker, came into the room. She held a .32 caliber revolver, casually, in her gloved hand. She was wearing a perfume that gave off the scent of sandalwood.

"*Oy*, what a bellicose family," observed Groucho. "There ought to be a suitable pun to go with 'bellicose,' but my powers of invention seem to have fled."

"You assholes," accused Alicia, coming farther into the big office. "If you hadn't dug up Doug's body, we wouldn't have to get rid of you now. That was stupid."

"We were curious," said Groucho, "to find out why Spellman was blackmailing you, dear lady."

Jack said, "He happened to be here the night Alicia lost her temper."

"Lost her temper is a polite way of putting it," I said. "She shot the guy dead."

"He was going to walk out on me," explained Alicia. "Naturally I got angry. I don't like being dumped."

"Or being blackmailed," I said.

"Spellman was a bastard, with no loyalty whatsoever," said Jack. "Here he was portraying Ty-Gor, and yet he had the nerve to—"

"We don't think he tried to blackmail your sister," said Groucho, "until your father began to pressure Warlock to fire him."

"Randy was fooling around with my stupid stepmother," said Alicia. "It was so obvious that even Dad noticed it."

"Spellman wanted us to guarantee him the part, or he'd send some pictures he'd taken to the police," added her brother.

Alicia said, "But we couldn't put pressure on Dad without having to tell him what Randy was blackmailing us about."

"This saga of family woes brings tears to my eyes, kids," said Groucho. "But let us pause for a moment while I reiterate that doing away with us won't be as easy as removing Doug Cahan was."

"Or Randy Spellman," I added.

"They'll never tie us in with that one," Alicia told me, her smile dark and smug. "They're still looking for Dorothy Woodrow. Jack and I fixed that up."

"The reason we're being this frank with you," said her brother, tapping the stock of his rifle, "is that you won't be alive much longer and it doesn't matter."

"Here's my notion of how you worked it," said Groucho. "Jack went openly onto the Warlock lot the day of the killing. He sent a fake note from Spellman to Dorothy, probably something about his needing to talk to her about their blackmail enterprises."

"Sure," admitted Jack. "We knew she was helping him. That's why we decided to frame her."

"And your dear sister most likely smuggled herself into the studio by hiding out in the truck that delivered the palm trees," continued Groucho. "After she killed Spellman and planted the threatening note, she hightailed it over the rear wall and was picked up by you."

Alicia laughed. "Bingo, that's just about what happened. You're smarter than you look, Groucho."

"I take that as a compliment."

Jack glanced up at the clock on the office wall. "Let's get on with it, Sis. I'll shoot these trespassers."

"Put your guns aside, both of you." Arthur Wright Benson appeared in the doorway. Unlike his offspring, he wasn't carrying a weapon.

Jack scowled at his father. "Dad, we have to kill them," he pleaded. "Otherwise, the honor of the Benson family—"

"The Benson family hasn't had much in the way of honor for

quite a while now." The author stepped into his office. "I suppose this sounds funny under the circumstances, gentlemen. But I do apologize for my children."

"Father, just go back to the house," said Alicia, anger in her voice. "Jack and I are capable of handling—"

"Yes, I know, dear. Capable of handling them the way you handled Doug and Randy."

"You've been out in the hall eavesdropping," accused his son. "Everything we've done was for the—"

"What did you do with the fifteen thousand dollars, Alicia?"

"I have a lot of expenses, and your allowance to me has always been—"

"Give me the revolver." Benson held out his hand. "I imagine the police will want it."

"I won't. I'm going to—"

"Hand it to me. Now!"

She pressed her lips together tightly, then pouted. She exhaled through her nose, glaring at her father. "Here," she said in a small, thin voice, and slapped the gun into her father's palm.

"That's a good girl." Benson dropped the revolver into his coat pocket. "You, too, Jack. Lay the rifle on the floor and step away from it."

"Dad, if these two live, it will destroy your reputation. They'll tell the papers about Alicia and me and—"

"No, my reputation will survive," Benson told him. "Certainly my readers will be shocked and surprised to learn that I've fathered two murderers, but they'll remain loyal to Ty-Gor."

"Fuck Ty-Gor," said Jack. But he placed the rifle carefully down on the tan carpeting.

Benson said to me, "Will you call the police, Mr. Denby?"

"I already have," I said.

Twenty-nine

Two of the deputies took Alicia and Jack Benson away into the misty night. Three others ventured into the jungle to find what was left of Doug Cahan. Groucho went along to lead them to the site, explaining that he'd been one of the original founders of the Boy Scouts of America and was a crackerjack tracker. "Or possibly a trackerjack cracker, but one of those at the very least," he'd told them.

Meantime I made use of a smaller office in the Arthur Wright Benson, Inc., building to do some telephoning.

Old Benson remained in his office, calling his attorneys.

First off, I called home.

"Jane Danner studio," answered Myra.

"Howdy, miss, this is the president of the Oxnard Hollywood Molly Fan Club," I said. "We're in town, and how would it be if all twenty-seven of us dropped over for autographs and possibly lots of glazed donuts?"

"She's right here, Mr. Denby. Hold on."

My wife asked, "Have you been injured in any way?"

"Not at all. I merely wanted to inform you that I'm going to be late."

"So what happened?"

"Well, I didn't get hit on the head."

"Besides that."

I told her about finding the missing accountant, being tracked through the fog-ridden jungles, establishing who'd murdered Randy Spellman, and summoning the local law.

She said, "Those nitwits might've shot you, Frank."

"Such was their intention, but they failed," I pointed out. "By hiding in the trees we lost Jack Benson for a spell, and then Arthur Wright Benson dropped by in the nick of time."

"What it comes down to is that Dorothy Woodrow is in the clear as far as the murder of Spellman goes."

"Sure, but that's not going to mean much to Enery."

"She was involved in Spellman's blackmailing game," said Jane. "That may still mean trouble for her."

"Whether it does or not, I don't think she's going to keep up her romance with him," I said. "My problem is, I keep getting movies and real life mixed up. So I was hoping for a happy ending."

"We'll have to settle for a not-too-miserable ending."

"Afraid so. Are you in shipshape condition?"

"A few cramps, but otherwise hunky-dory."

"Good, I'll be home as soon as I can. Bye, Love."

"Same here."

I next called Mitch Tandofsky's home number.

"What?" my Studio City police friend answered. I heard what sounded like an Artie Shaw band remote broadcast playing in the background.

"I didn't know you were a swing fan, Mitch."

"Sure, I'm a hep cat. Was that what you called to find out, Frank?"

"No, I wanted to inform you, old buddy, that you ought to get in touch with the sheriff's substation near Rancho Tygoro," I said. "Alicia Benson and her brother, Jack, have been arrested on suspicion of murder. She knocked off a missing bookkeeper named Doug Cahan *and* the late Randy Spellman. Her brother lent aid and comfort in various ways."

He produced a dejected sound. "I suppose you and your comedian friend solved the whole thing?"

"A good part of it, although the Benson kids filled in a lot of details."

"They confessed?"

"Only because they were planning to add us to the list of victims." I went on to tell him how Arthur Wright Benson had stepped in to come to our rescue.

"You guys ought to do a turn on *The Amateur Hour*," Tandofsky said. "But I guess as amateur detectives you're not bad. Thanks, Frank. Good night."

Next, I called Larry Shell to suggest he might get some nice pictures for the *LA Times* if he got over to the sheriff's place. And I left a message with May Sankowitz's answering service with enough details to provide her with some items for her various Hollywood gossip outlets.

When I stepped into the hallway, Groucho was slouching my way. I noticed both of his trouser knees were muddy. "Why's that?"

"Even expert trackers stumble now and then, as Confucius often remarked," Groucho said, rubbing at one damp knee. "In fact, he took to saying it so often that we quit inviting him to our tea dances. That turned out to be a mistake, since he was the one supplying the tea. However—"

"What say we take our leave?" I asked.

195

Shall I bring the car to a full stop?" enquired Groucho. "Or would you prefer to make a dramatic leap as I merely slow down to fifty miles an hour?"

"I'm a little weary tonight," I said as the Cadillac entered our block. "You might as well stop."

The night fog was heavy, and the lighted windows of our house were fuzzy yellow rectangles. From the Pacific came the hollow moan of a lone foghorn.

Groucho hit the brakes. "We still have a collection of loose ends, Rollo," he said. "Notably the fate of Dorothy Woodrow."

"Once she hears she's not a suspect in Spellman's murder, she'll come out of hiding."

"Probably so, since the two Benson tots aren't likely to talk about being blackmailed."

"They're going to be indicted for Doug Cahan's murder first, most likely." I opened my door and almost yawned. "Could be a while before they go to trial for knocking off Randy. If ever."

"Quite true."

I stood on the foggy sidewalk near his open window. "I'll call you tomorrow." This time I yawned fully.

"Best wait until the chariot of Apollo lights the sky," he advised. "And in our neighborhood Apollo doesn't go over until about midday. That'll give me time to catch up on my insomnia. Farewell." He drove away.

Letting myself into the house, I was greeted, quietly but enthusiastically, by Dorgan. He came padding out of Jane's studio making low pleased noises.

Myra followed. "Jane turned in about an hour ago, Mr. Denby."

"She's okay?"

"Yes, the cramps didn't last long. She's fine now."

"I'm glad you could stay until I got back."

"Hey, I'm glad to," she said, getting her coat on. "Besides, Jane pays me overtime wages."

"Yes, I believe that was also what kept Florence Nightingale in the field for so long," I said. "See you tomorrow."

After Jane's assistant had left and I'd bent to massage Dorgan's belly, I went quietly into our bedroom.

Jane, not fully awake, said, "Are you sure you didn't get hit on the head again?" in a small, blurred voice.

"Absolutely. You can feel my head if you'd care to."

But she was already asleep.

Thirty

When Dorgan and I returned from our morning stroll, Jane met us in the doorway. "You were right," she said.

"About what exactly?"

"Dorothy Woodrow."

After snuffling around my wife's legs, our bloodhound entered the living room.

Jane and I followed. "Dorothy telephoned?"

"A few minutes ago." Jane continued on into the kitchen. "Now that she knows they don't want her for murder, she's getting ready to reappear. She wants to see you first, though."

It was commencing to grow bright and sunny in there. Coffee was perking. "Where is she?"

"At her place in Manhattan Beach." Jane took two cups off their hooks in the cupboard, set them on the table. "She'd like you to go over there. She wants to talk to you."

"I take it she doesn't want me to bring Enery along?"

She took the coffeepot off the burner, brought it to the table, and poured. "Dorothy went so far as to say she didn't even want you to tell him where she is," Jane replied. "You going to go?"

"Yeah, it's something I'd better do."

Jane sat down, rested her folded hands on the table near her coffee cup. "I was the one who urged you and Groucho to get involved with this case in the first place," she said. "It hasn't, you know, turned out the way I expected."

"Well, it was never going to turn out very well for Enery," I said, sitting across the table from her. "But we didn't know that much about Dorothy then. Anyway, we did find out who killed Randy Spellman."

"That's important," she said. "I suppose."

"Sure, and the cause of justice has been served."

"Phooey," Jane said, "is how I sum it all up."

Dorothy Woodrow lived in a small white stucco house about a half mile from the Pacific. The street was narrow, and an old Blue Ford missing a rear tire was dying in the weedy driveway next door. The grass had grown up about running-board-high all around it, and a sooty seagull was perched on the hood.

A light rain had been falling ever since I got to the town of Manhattan Beach. I parked next to a stretch of curb that had Dorothy's address number stenciled on it, got out, and jumped across a muddy flower border.

Three long-ago-painted red steps led up to the orange door.

As I raised my hand to knock, the door opened.

"I'm glad you could make it, Frank." Dorothy was wearing jeans and a candy-stripe shirt. Her blonde hair was pulled back, and she wore no makeup. "You didn't tell Enery I was back here, did you?"

"Nope." I followed her down a narrow pale yellow hall, into a small parlor.

"The phone's been ringing a hell of a lot, but I'm not answering," she said. "Can I get you something to drink?"

"No, thanks. You wanted to talk to me."

She lowered herself onto a narrow tan sofa. Attached to the wall behind it with red-headed pushpins was a large bullfight poster. The matador had just thrust his sword into the bull.

"What do you think," the young woman asked, "is going to happen?"

"Well, first off," I answered, sitting in a slightly lopsided white wicker chair, "Alicia Benson's going to be tried for murdering Doug Cahan. Eventually they may also charge her with killing Randy Spellman. It all depends on—"

"I know all that, Frank. I heard it on the radio, then read it in the papers," Dorothy said in a tired voice. "That's why I came back home. What I meant was—what the hell is going to happen to *me?*"

"Alicia and Jack Benson know you were working with Randy on his blackmail racket," I told her. "That's how they were able to lure you to his trailer that night. The story you gave us wasn't altogether true. The note they faked had something to do with Randy wanting to see you about business, didn't it?"

She sighed. "Yes, I made up some parts of my story," she admitted. "Enery never knew I was still involved with Randy or what was going on. See, I didn't want to hurt the poor guy."

"Oh, I can sense that, yeah."

"No, honestly, Frank. I really liked Enery," she said.

"That sounds like so much bullshit to me," I observed. "Though maybe Enery, who seems to be in love with you, will buy it."

"It doesn't matter, since I've decided not to see him from now on," Dorothy said, resting her palms on her knees. "But you'd be doing me a terrific favor, Frank, if you'd' tell him that I'm sorry about all—"

"No, nope. I won't deliver any more messages for you."

"Look, I was involved in helping Randy blackmail people," she said. "But keep in mind that every damned one of them had done something that was—"

"Hey, you don't have to convince me of anything." I stood up. "Groucho and I figure you were also the one who went to Randy's ex-wife's place to look for more of his blackmail files. A stuntwoman could dive out that high window with no trouble. Even one with a bum leg."

"If I was going to carry on the business, I needed all the material I—"

"I will be talking to Enery, since he's a friend of mine," I cut in. "When I tell him about your part in all this, you probably won't have to worry about him anymore."

"No, I don't want him to know I was—"

"Too late."

Dorothy got up from the sofa. "If it gets out that I was Randy's partner, will the cops come after me, do you think?"

I moved into the hall. "Maybe you ought to talk to a lawyer."

She gave me a thin smile. "I know what's really bothering you," she said. "You and Groucho both. You thought I was sweet and innocent, then you found out that I'm not quite as nice as you'd imagined. That's what's got you pissed off."

"That could be part of it."

"I didn't kill Randy or anybody else." She walked beside me down the yellow hall. "The Bensons tried to frame me. Alicia is as crazy as a—"

"Talk to a lawyer," I repeated, and I left her house.

The rain had grown colder and more persistent.

Thirty-one

Ty-Gor was tied to a stake in the center of the cannibal village. About twenty feet away a dozen very belligerent natives were beating on large primitive drums. Enery McBride, wearing a lion-skin loincloth, an ornate feathered headdress, and a necklace of fake human teeth, was seated upon a large throne that was supposed to have been carved from raw stone.

"You will now be sacrificed to the devil god," he said, pointing at the captive jungle king.

Beside Enery a gaunt witch doctor, wearing an outfit made of an imitation zebra skin and some real ostrich plumes, bent close to whisper in his ear.

"And then, white trespasser, you shall provide a meal for my warriors," added Enery in a booming voice.

Standing just to the rear of the script girl, I winced. The dialogue for this sequence hadn't been brilliant from the start, yet somebody else, probably the erstwhile pulp writer Wallace Deems, had added the "white trespasser" part. But I had to admit to myself that "you shall provide a meal for my warriors" was all mine.

The director, Joshua Borkman, was moving uneasily in his

canvas chair. A thickset man of fifty, he was one of those directors who actually wore riding breeches and boots. He was glaring now at Carl Nesbit, our new Ty-Gor.

Finally, with an exasperated snort, he jumped to his feet. "Cut," he hollered. "Why the hell are you making those funny faces, Carl?"

"Sorry," the actor apologized. "It's my chest."

"And what is wrong with your frigging chest, Carl?"

"It itches," explained the new Ty-Gor. "They shaved all the hair off and then slapped pancake makeup all over, and . . ." He shrugged as best he could while lashed to a pole. "It itches, but I can't scratch."

"Stanley," shouted the director. "Do something. Fix his goddamn chest. We'll try this dim-witted scene again in fifteen." He went striding off toward another part of the soundstage as a makeup man and his assistant came hurrying over.

I headed over to Enery's throne, stepping around cameras and over cables. "What's on the menu today besides Ty-Gor?"

"Hi, Frank," he said, leaving the throne. "I'm not in a very good mood."

"So I imagined."

"But I am glad Dorothy isn't suspected of killing Spellman," he said. "You and Groucho did a swell job of tracking down these Bensons."

"Part of the time they were tracking us."

"Do you know where she is?"

"Yeah, but I don't think Dorothy wants to—"

"I know, Frank," Enery said as we walked clear of the cannibal village set. "She hasn't called me since the news broke that the Bensons had—allegedly—done Randy in and that she was off the hook. You don't have to be a master detective to figure out what that means."

"Nope, it's obvious she's ready to move on, Enery."

He toyed with his dental necklace. "I knew she was . . . restless. But I didn't expect it would happen this soon. And maybe I had the idea I was going to be the exception." When he gave a sad shake of his head, a feather floated free of his chieftain headdress. "Still, I'm going to miss her."

"Enery, you ought to . . ." I was having trouble with this.

"Ought to what? Get over her. Sure, I'll—"

"Know what she was really up to," I said. "It's true she didn't kill Spellman. The Bensons tried to frame her for that, and she's innocent. But—"

"I know that. It's in the newspaper." He was frowning at me.

"It's possible that none of this other stuff will ever come out," I continued.

"Stuff about Dorothy?" He put his hand on my shoulder.

"Groucho and I found out that she was still involved with Spellman."

"No, she swore to me that she—"

"Not sleeping with him," I said, although I wasn't even sure that was true. "But helping him work his blackmail racket. That's really why the Bensons tried to frame her, to get rid of her and Randy at the same time."

He stopped and put his other hand on my other shoulder and turned me toward him. Frowning more deeply, he asked, "You guys are sure of this?"

"Yeah. After Spellman was killed, she even broke in on his former wife's place looking for some of his blackmail files," I told him. "And—well, I had a talk with her a few hours ago, and she admitted she was in it with him."

"You saw her? Where is she?"

"You don't want to see her," I said quietly. "More important, she doesn't want to see you."

He sat down in a stray canvas chair. "Jesus, this is tough to believe, Frank," he said. "I'm starting to think I was an even bigger sap than I realized."

"Dorothy was fond of you," I said. "For a while anyway. But she didn't want to give up the blackmail. It looks like Arnie Carr, her ventriloquist friend, was going to help her carry on."

My friend held up his hand in a stop-now gesture. "Okay, Frank, I guess that's all I have to hear right now," he said. "I better get back over to my throne, we're going to start shooting again pretty soon."

"I'm sorry things—"

"That's okay. You and Groucho did what I asked you to do," he said, rising up. "Not your fault you dug up more truth than I wanted."

We started walking back to the cannibal village.

When we got close, an assistant script girl waved at me. "Frank, there's an emergency call for you," she said. "From your home."

"Is my wife all right?"

"Yes, but her assistant wants to talk to you."

"I'll see you, Enery."

"Take it easy," he advised.

I hurried away in the direction in which the young woman had pointed.

*   *   *

A plug-in phone was sitting on a small table in a dim-lit part of Soundstage 3.

"This is Frank Denby," I said, nervous.

"It's okay, Mr. Denby. This is Myra," said my wife's assistant.

"Is Jane all right?"

"Yes, but the contractions have started up, and they've been coming every few minutes." she told me in an excited voice. "I telephoned Dr. Mazoujian, and he says to get her over to the hospital."

"Help her get ready," I said. "I'll be there in less than an hour and—"

"Jane doesn't think she can wait that long, Mr. Denby," said Myra. "So I'm going to drive her over now. She'll be at Bayside Memorial Hospital. Okay?"

"Yeah, I'll leave right now. Can I talk to Jane?"

"Just a minute. She's been packing an overnight bag. Hold on."

I noticed I'd been inhaling and exhaling through my mouth. I also felt a little dizzy.

After what seemed like a long time, Jane came on the phone. "Drive carefully, Frank. Relax. I'm doing as well as can be expected."

"I shouldn't have left you there when—"

"Our daughter's early. Not your fault," she said. "Okay, I'll see you at the hospital."

"Soon as I can get there. I love you."

"I knew that."

As I was hurrying for the exit, Enery caught up with me. "Trouble?" he asked.

"The stork," I answered, not slowing down.

"That's great. Good luck."

I popped out into the gray, rainy afternoon.

Thirty-two

It wasn't raining in Bayside.

I parked across the street from the hospital—a Southern California sort of hospital. It was three stories high, with peach-colored stucco walls and slanting roofs of red tile. There were many palm tress decorating its wide front lawn.

Running up to the glass doorways, I splashed in at least three puddles.

In the lobby I had to dodge to keep from colliding with a very pale woman in a wheelchair.

She was saying to the younger woman behind her chair, "He should've been here by now. He knows when I'm getting released."

"You know Uncle Lowell, Mom."

"That's what's worrying me."

I'd been to the Bayside Memorial Hospital before, so I knew exactly where the Maternity Ward was located.

Although I'd never actually been in a Maternity Ward waiting room before, the one I now found myself in seemed familiar.

That was probably because it resembled most of the waiting rooms in the dozens of hospital movies I'd seen over the years. There were three other husbands sharing this one with me. One fellow, who was pacing and chain-smoking, looked to be a few years younger than I was. The other two, older and more relaxed, sat calmly reading from the collection of vintage copies of the *Saturday Evening Post, Liberty, Life,* and *Collier's.*

If the young expectant father hadn't already staked out the pacing space, I would probably have been pacing myself. Sitting, I failed to get through three separate short-short stories in three different back issues of *Collier's.* I was too restless even to read all the way through the longer cartoon captions. I checked my wristwatch at least once every two minutes.

"Your first kid?" one of the relaxed fathers inquired. He had black curly hair and a good start toward a second chin.

"It is, yes. Yours?"

"First one with this wife," he answered. "Two with my first wife. Things'll go better if you relax."

After looking again at my watch, I said, "That's good advice, except—"

"Mr. Denby?" asked the slim, middle-aged nurse who had come into the smoky waiting room.

"Here!" I popped up out of my chair, shedding the several vintage magazines from my lap. "Is there anything wrong?"

She smiled a patient smile. "Your wife is out of the delivery room," she said. "And you're the father of a baby girl."

"What about *my* wife?" asked the pacer.

"No news yet, Mr. Reisberson," the nurse told him. "If you'll come along with me, Mr. Denby, you can view your daughter. And in just a bit you'll be able to see your wife."

I asked, following the nurse, "They're both all right?"

"Yes, both of them are fine. Your daughter weighs six and a half pounds."

The two relaxed expectant fathers smiled at me. The curly-haired one said, "Congratulations, buddy."

The nervous father went right on pacing and smoking.

On the other side of the large glass viewing window, a different nurse was holding a baby. She pointed at the blanket-wrapped baby and then toward me.

From what I could see, my nose pressing to the glass, our daughter was exceptionally cute and already had a sprinkling of dark curly hair. I didn't pay much attention to the other newborn babies who were resting in the three rows of cribs.

As I watched, the nurse placed our baby in one of the empty cribs.

"Don't settle on that one until you've seen all the rest, Rollo."

Turning briefly away from my daughter, I noticed Groucho standing just to my right. "Too late, we've decided on this one," I said. "Besides, she's the best-looking of the lot. How'd you know I was here, Groucho?"

"I phoned your domicile, and Jane's assistant, after shamelessly flirting with me, told me what was in the wind," he explained. "I'm glad she did, because the only thing that I knew was in the wind was a rather shabby kite and a few—"

"Our baby is a girl," I cut in.

"Ah, just as Jane foretold." He sighed. "Then I fear there's little chance of your naming your offspring Groucho."

"I'd estimate none at all, actually." I was again watching our daughter's crib. "Jane's pretty much decided on naming her Jillian."

"With a *G* or *J*?"

"*J.*"

"Cheer up then, Rollo, that's not that far from Julius."

"Far enough."

"Tell your missus that I approve of Jillian as a name," Groucho said. "I'll show my appreciation with a suitable gift to commemorate the occasion. In fact, if I can get to the five-and-ten-cent store before it closes, I'll pick you out a suitable gift this very day."

What do you think?"

"Best-looking baby on the West Coast."

"Not in the whole darned United States?"

"I'd have to get a closer look at her before committing myself." Jane, propped up with two pillows, was sitting up in her hospital bed. I was standing beside the bed, holding her hand.

"They'll be bringing her in here soon," my wife said.

"Dr. Mazoujian told me she's fine," I said. "And you're fine, too."

"Well, that's fine," said Jane.

Leaning, I kissed her. "I'm going to try not to get involved with any more murder cases for the immediate future," I promised. "Therefore, you don't have to worry about my getting conked on the head."

"You're sure you won't miss being slugged? It's become such a part of your life."

To switch the conversation from my tendency to get sapped, I said, "Groucho dropped by the hospital. He thinks Jillian is a terrific name, and he says he'll be sending us a present."

"What sort of present? Another dog, do you think?"

"Not unless they sell dogs at Woolworth's. Groucho is—"

At that point a nurse entered the room, bringing in our new daughter.